XEROX
OVER
MANHATTAN

XEROX OVER MANHATTAN

SHANE JESSE CHRISTMASS

Apocalypse Party

Xerox Over Manhattan

ISBN-13: 978-1-7335694-0-8
ISBN-10: 1-7335694-0-5

Cover design by Matthew Revert

www.apocalypse-party.com

Printed in the U.S.A

Your extreme shyness. Your supple feet in green heels. President Ricky's morbid obsession with dirty underlinen. His yawning in morning then tobacco cough. Camera pans around remote regions of Midwest. Dead faces disturb President Ricky. Black perforated scabs. His skull hairless. Crisp skin. Scorched lovers. A man in a straightjacket. A vase of flowers. Xerox machine over Manhattan. You hand out photocopies at my funeral. I take my lunch at the McDonalds on Eighth Avenue between 34th and 35th Streets. I steer clear of hospital food. I'm heavily into you. You ask me if this is okay. I close my eyes. A heated conversation takes place. You turned up one warm summer night. We went off and dug up skulls at Potter's Field. We made a bonfire. We put pentagrams in chalk on the sidewalk. You took a beating. I sleep in your apartment. I sleep with a butterfly knife under my pillow. You sleep on the floor. I throw the butterfly knife into the East River. I also throw seven bags of speed as well. You take me out to dinner. We go sit in a Baptist Church out in New Jersey. A bum asks us for a few dollars. Nothing is playing on the car radio. I give you $100 for the pentagram medallion around your neck. Young man keeps his tassel loafers in a small black box. Stasis effect among people in the street. They are grotesque figures. Dead men scooped from the mournful sea. Salesman selling wallpaper from suitcases. Long underwear held together with Scotch tape. Bible knowledge about the existence of another Earth. Bird refuge on the islands of Indonesia. Bright brochures with full-colour photos left behind in a briefcase. Arithmetic scribbled into a notebook.

Theoretical physics. Medical specialists. Clergymen in control of sewage-disposal systems. New food sources from rotten produce. I disconnect the saline bag. The telephone lines vibrate. Watching the inferno that is Manhattan burn. Your eyes are light and cold, gaping open wide. Clear fluid weeps from your wound. A small trapdoor. Sweat forms a sheen. Shock treatment again. A tire jack across the back of my skull. Birth-control plans for first world countries. Government bureaus firebombed by Siberian tribesman. Dry lips in the Gobi Desert. Circuits malfunction on the JUQUEEN. Hand weapons with radiant switches. Handguns with small dials. You bath in a wide beam of sunlight. Bodies in a dump truck heading to Potter's Field. Corpses pour into muddy holes. Heads bashed by shovels, high schools converted to torture yards. Subjection to primal law. Teeth into a tiny mouse. The clanging of a gong. You lift your head from the pillow. Her voice hoarse. Batons and rubber bullets. Protective screen over the biosphere. Metabolism techniques destroying thyroid health. The cold blue eyes in your DMV photo. Suicide attempt during Ibogaine treatments. You have animal intellect. Interactive display inside a plywood tree. Inferior genes pushed into an empty space. Your black eyes inside a cobalt body. Autumn is President Ricky's favourite season. President Ricky purchases a swivel chair for the secretarial desk. Light conversation conducted via headset. Outside entrance leads to the switchboard cubicle. Burnt ossicle in your middle ear. Transmission of pressure through the cochlea. The logical apparatuses required for phone sex include sleepless nights,

Coca-Cola and cardio-respiratory failure. You have bloodless lips. You sleep within restless oceans. Index finger releases the safety catch on the handgun. Car polish. Sunrise over NYC. Drinks are delivered to our table. Drinks happy in our guts. Electric blanket on low setting. Chef boiling a big pot of noodles. All this occurs afterhours. You notice the rope burns around my neck. Handshakes. Small black eye for wearing a powder-blue pant suit. A small black box that houses a cylindrical instrument. Faint vibration from the instrument. Nudists in the Gymnasium, undated photographs, 1930s jigsaw pieces all over the sauna, barf on the tiles. Teeth. Below me the underpasses, under me the concrete, bitumen of the freeways. A fog bank over Hudson River. Animals and glass objects. People dying. Insults. Knives. A car lingers downtown. You go lay down on the floor. Window glass smashes. I reach for a wine glass. You sleep in the fetal position beside educated men. At the porter's desk in the corridor of the main building, a woman sits. She edits and redacts confidential documents. Her ears bleed. Several empty glasses of Spanish Brandy. I take a seat on a bus heading to Carnegie Hill. I turn slowly and look at street signs, advertisements, hoardings, bubble-gummed side streets, and suicide orders. I roll in the backseat of the taxi. Hand sweat on rock walls. You're asleep in small boats. From your back muscles, sweat pours. Machine-like precision to destroy you. Magazine publishers talking to television stations. Cadillacs, Chevrolets and Chryslers appear from murky blackness. Complex espionage devices installed in the cobblestone driveway by order of President

Ricky. Sleepless nights enclosed in overhead cables. Encephalic disturbances in the high imagination of President Ricky. You investigate your fatal coma. You investigate the permanent neurological after-effects of that fatal coma. President Ricky wraps his chubby fingers around the therapeutic facilities. His writhes in heat stroke and sober voice. You fall onto the bed. You kick the nightstand away. Shoe leather fills your nostrils. President Ricky was someone's husband once. Blood drizzles from a wound. The angular fingers of President Ricky over your breasts and wet crevices. Hands like a clinical practice. Spiral staircases all throughout Chicago. A morgue team collecting cell organisms. Electronic diathermy in a large town's orphanage. An insane gleam to your eyes. Erotic appointments factored into the travel itinerary. President Ricky sings. Twilight. His demented head. He cries and laughs. Blood on my jaw line. My hands on the table. I push rigid for some reason. Ice drowning in the whirlpool. I breathe in. President Ricky slides. Something prods the skin beneath my shirt pocket. I smile. My eyes ache. Ten minutes before a light sleep. President Ricky turns and drives off in a Toyota. He leaps from sandcastle to sandcastle. I thin to gloominess. Strong whisky held by steady hands, poured from a crystal decanter. Handgun on a wide desk. Mammalian emotion inside the colony walls. The orb of a periscope. You ejaculate onto my middle finger. The pungent scent of your pretty face. The unpleasant taste of salmonella poisoning during sex act. Vice murmurs during steamy bath. The shiny shoes of robots. Urinary infections and dope smoking. The obliteration of your subcutaneous tissues. Needle-beam lasers fire from under the Atlantic Ocean. Electronic reflex across cyborg membranes. Red eyes of a faceless evil being. Handguns. Portable lasers. Hand weapons. Neck muscles of a yellowish green body. Transparent casing on carnivorous animals; their vital organs exposed. The reptilian body of fire-worshippers. Corpses in the charnel house. Vengeance plans for total damnation. We found envelopes and letters at Dead Horse Bay. The handwriting was indecipherable, ink attached, nothing more. I walk to the front door of the apartment. You had opened it before me. I can make out your cheekbones. I stare at you. You bellow. You take out a whip. You're not crazy. A carded package of cosmetics on the kitchen table. Your nose crinkles. I fall out of bed, out into the corridor. You approach me. Children in East River Park. Cement inside an unperformed car. Gasoline poured through bullet holes. Projected on the screen at the Paris Theatre, a nasty-looking man. Where are his shoes? The man walks. He mills around the outside of a dance studio. His tongue skilled in providing pleasure. Plastic doors. People rush about. You feed on the bedlam. A stray dog screeches. Fainting looks at subway cars. I grab a New York Post. You pull the tail of my shirt. You withdraw further. Noises. A sports bag full of handguns. Hospital tests to measure President Ricky's mood. Videotape capturing everyday violence. Contamination of consumer society. Wet shroud over the bus door. Taxis escorting tourists around. Transplanted organs incurring psychotic symptoms. Blood out of the skin opening. Digital distractions. Sexual neighbours. Excessive noise. Cabin cruiser with a refurbished cockpit. In the fog of night your face has pig's eyes. An old piano has a suicide note where the sheet music should be. A close shot of a bonfire and medicine bottles. Your attorney visits the police headquarters. He's a dark-haired young man. The thunder frightens you. Painted boats. Overhanging flesh. Miscellaneous items. Mists. Dust. Remember this encounter. You're on a waterbed. I end up living with you. Symptoms of psychosis. Electricity. Paranoia. My poor eyesight. You're in the hotel gym. You contain thick brown hair and almond eyes. President Ricky and I are in another room. I despise him. He has everything. He drops everything. He nods once. He giggles nervously. President Ricky is afraid of his shoes. A train pulls in. It's ten minutes late. Dogs turn up. President Ricky hands me a plastic cup. I have to talk to him. He's contesting with poltergeists. He contracts whooping cough. We walk past the service elevators. I'm cloaked in extreme darkness. President Ricky has a radio attached to his belt. He lives in a foxhole. It's above a volcanic cleft. Brimstone in lozenge shapes. Body at right angles. Cancer patients. You push yourself against my skin. You murmur, remembering to the point of dread. I look at my lit cigarette. Asteroid belts. Complex organisms. Sociopaths in Point Morris. Sack-loads of porn. Hopeless agony inside an inhuman fiend. Stomach covered in cum. A large flat rock in the middle of West 54th Street. A woman's body in Rudy's Bar & Grill connected to life support equipment. A cell phone rings in empty darkness. A Ford sedan full of cash earnings stolen from Hathaway's Diner in Cincinnati, Ohio. An eerie croon from mountain caves. The slim waist of hand models. The utter terror of paper dolls. Water in the kettle boiling. The leather belt around her waist is singed from cigarette burns. You open up your body and leap, spin, hang in tatters from the ceiling beams. Stuffed animals on the table. Sweat as the shadow blots. Swollen carcasses in Brooklyn Hospital Centre. Two people living inside your body. Someone inside outshined by the external you. Thai food on Eighth Avenue. NYPD state that a Babies 'R' Us employee took a photo up a woman's dress while working at the store. You take a swim in the Hudson River. Pale illumination and the sweet stink of the seawater. You penetrate my ass. You roll cigarettes between the screams. Stupid dreams from the morgue keeper. Special investigators with their high-octane corpuscles and black eyes. President Ricky transported to police station on a second-degree theft charge. You practice ESP to converse with him. Tight shot. Close up. President Ricky's mug shot. Your nervous system buried in cocaine deals and overpowering laughing. Language spoken in small beliefs and heartbeats. Your substance intake makes for psychotic disorder and bad moustaches. Your keen eyes on all the banknotes. The unique form of the small-scale model that details President Ricky's new compound. Homosexual publications detailing drug addiction. You draw a deep breath inside the subway. A 300 pound monster is up for execution. A flashlight beam on shoe leather. Upon the pavement a shrill whistle. The rough tug of a t-shirt from your shoulders. Children on the basketball court. Tepid water in the Bronx Kill. Your eyes. An upstate campsite closed for cleaning. The proprietor having a rest. You're out on the balcony. The wastebasket full of bloodied tissues. Dirty looks. Tooth and bone. The sun-greeting ground. Noxious smoke over Midtown. My shoelaces undone. Quinine in the supply room. A drink dispenser outside the elevator. A knock on our hotel door. Hectic sex. My anorexic waist. You breathlessly. Steadily we're on West 14th Street. The steward whispers into the microphone. The oily carnage of the East River. Giant shots of Brandy. Your blood ceases. Thick eyeglasses beneath a blonde wig. My overdone makeup. Black teeth caused by Scarsdale diet and LSD intake. You restrain me on the floor. Sweat forms on my skin. Alcohol poured over brain implants. I take a sip. Xanax and brown eggnog. You press a strange device against my sternum. Plastic bags full of Max Factor products. Murmurs in your veins. You're drunk and falling down. Bubble bath and liquid teeth. Adrenalin rush through your whole body. Memory and forgetting. Body in the trunk of your car. Brain implants. IV drip. Windscreen wipers. The vice-soaked isolation on Monticello. A hideous death and the body had black hair. Nude shapes make tearless sobs. Fortress-like apartment in Washington Heights. A gas tank under the stairs. The floor is covered in tobacco and sawdust. I sit slowly, reluctantly, folding the entrance fee and free ticket into my pocket. President Ricky licks my skin, leaving a blue mark. Campaign rallies held from abandoned aqueducts. I wallow in a humid substance. EEG again. We were wearing rat costumes. It was Christmas.

The road was a long stretch somewhere upstate. At first I heard you moaning, I was wiping the blood away with a toilet roll. Water dripped from the latrine. Nobody wanted to work with me. Eventually the driver came back. I left messages on the answering machine. I wanted to see NYC again, and then sleep. Rest in the robust mound of living. My jeans on the worktable. President Ricky pushes through a glass door. He buys me lingerie. He causes people to be aggressive. President Ricky develops psychosis. He places me in the backroom. He puts his arm around me. He pumps me full of monoxide, carbon dioxide. Symptoms persist for days. I watch him drop onto the bed. I thrust a rag into his mouth. A nauseous gateway for a larger sickness. Watercolours sprayed upon her cotton dress. Giant men wander through the dark evening. Lasers that are run on motor oil. Fashion models on television donating clothes to hurricane victims. The conception of Khloe Kardashian. Security guards protecting the member's area. Men's shoes used as weapons in BDSM attacks. DNA taken from cigarette packets found in rubbish bins. President Ricky finds himself broke, walking in clear cold windless afternoons. He photoshoots all his false tasks and smokes some weed. He researches, with scientific intensity, the dull awe of secrecy and the hot impression of Hepatitis C. The seawater reflects the sky. Dead inhabitants, germs produced to grow into judges, sandy lungs, leather aprons. President Ricky doesn't have anyone he trusts. He mumbles. I ignore him. I'm tired of looking at him. I look at the ground. I place the key in the lock. I put a cold blanket on top of him. I shouldn't speculate about his diagnosis. I turn the television off. I should ensure that someone stays with him. I should lockdown the bedroom. The door closes. It is locked. I am forgetful. Plumes of soot on the bedspread. President Ricky has alabaster skin. He has hazel eyes. He breaks down. President Ricky stinks of Budweiser, Kools and tear-stained eyeliner. I can't comprehend his unclean attitude. President Ricky removes the bandages from his chest. The assault of corrective surgery. Implants made from plastic bags. You possess my firm mouth with red lips and warm laughter. The unseen menace in a dogged drug-market. Yellow eyes, worm-eaten eyes, a mouth full of tobacco juice and toothless gums. Girl with an animal growl who works as a spotter in Midtown Manhattan. The muscles of a middle-weight boxer emaciated by myasthenia gravis. Your yellow hair whipped with a silk handkerchief. Men without external sex organs. A sliced penis and scrotum in a coffee cup full of endocrine. Southern mansions repurposed into abortion clinics. Human hands in dark hallways. Worker plunges down elevator shaft in Brooklyn building. We meet in the lobby of the Gramercy Park Hotel. You primarily cope by shutting down your emotions. Manhattan. Empty stores. The familiar shuffles of subway platforms. Slow memories in my empty mind. My duffle bag full of Dendracin lotion. Plastic baskets of iodine. You decided to catch a train to Washington. It is two hours after your departure. You feel the earth around you. This ground isn't soft. Your coarse voice rises, and then falls in a ceaseless wave, it recognizes my bad mood. You become silent. You didn't go to

Washington. The movie camera has an underwater case. I cut a length of copper wire. You whisper in the darkness. You enter the inner room. The air is heavy. I dig into your skin. You bang your fist on the wall. You've had a haircut. Yu shut the door. You have bought a bottle of every kind of perfume. You purchase some long-distance electronics. I order double rum. A large squirrel in Central Park. Furry, its eyes are watching us, it has an inscrutable expression. You put your feet on my stomach. Your shout dies in a gurgle. President Ricky bathes in wine barrels in the basement of his apartment block. The hot impression of the light switch. President Ricky has small red eyes. He assembles precious stones that have greenish coils around them. President Ricky cuts his blunt nose. His hairpiece has grotesque wings. His eye sockets have reddish-brown fins. He sprints around the carpark with amazing speed. His imminent crash goes unhindered and he floats backward over asphalt and red grass. Luminous vegetation cover's President Ricky's reflective lenses. Happy smiles beneath the hairpiece. Nervous faces full of phosphorescence. Assassination notes written at frantic speeds. Warm vapours inside a large sinkhole. The complete perversion of North America. Woman grabs a newspaper. Plasma pours into subway grating. Train slowly pulls out from platform. Woman raises a large suitcase. Dark figures, who whistle badly, prowl the corridors of the police department. Perfume bottles inside cosmetic jars. Blank paper burns in an inhospitable atmosphere. Photographer outside the window pane. Camphor beneath your nose. A bulky newspaper being read by the bartender. The elevator boy makes enormous shadows. We meet in the lobby of the Gramercy Park Hotel. You primarily cope by shutting down your emotions. Manhattan. Empty stores. The familiar shuffles of subway platforms. Slow memories in my empty mind. My duffle bag full of Dendracin lotion. Plastic baskets of iodine. Woman grabs a newspaper. Plasma pours into subway grating. You call the meeting together. You suggest we wear masks for future meetings. I ask what colour they should be. It doesn't matter what colour they are. Cocaine and teeth gleaming. You insert the key into the lock. My lips. You ask me to interpret your dreams. You are clever. Shutdown at the East River Generating Station. You draw me an illustration of a man having a coronary. I'm sniffling in the Manhattan sun. I tell you I'm going to catch an Amtrak to Phoenix. Train slowly pulls out from platform. A woman squats over the pavement. A hurt woman with sore breasts. Long black hair in sharp photographic images. Unforgettable moments from these distant years. You take long absences to delve into deep thoughts. New machines on the Trans-Manhattan Expressway. Homosexual boys fuck the cruel bridegroom. You like mischievous laughter. You undress out of a black dinner dress. I wear your high heels. Light through the ventilating shaft. Scalpels into the skin. Destruction of the body with every body blow. Robots run for political office. Professional men tear down their immoral past. The possibility of fire hazards. An embankment of stones, almost a levee, holding back the seawater. Woman raises a large suitcase. Your spectral fingers smeared with newspaper ink. Hot temperature, police ponder burglary suspicions. Football skills on display in New Jersey. Stasis heart is not an intelligent organ. The Earth's gravitational field. The Earth's geomagnetic forecasting method is now in crisis. You come see, come via the Staten Island Ferry. Crates of rum on pontoons towed by the ferry. My limp cock in a leather mini-dress. Lipstick on your boxer shorts. Your body throbs with a sick feeling. Law enforcement slipping into black markets. European woman with a Chinese husband. Chinese husband discovers his shoe-fetishism while holidaying in London, and while in Germany for work. Husband's eyes. Woman's feet. Small army gathering in an ugly place. Passengers in bulletproof vests cause disruptive airplane flights. Countless species contracting mania and unproductive psychosis. The dark spaces in a horse's eyes. The magical spaces of abomination. President Ricky takes many notes. Weird shit discovered in colour photographs. A sample video file of nude men. Telephone numbers to subscribe to an online adult magazine. President Ricky calls, hungry to get the limited offer. A sexy centerfold selling valuable things. Sunny postcards from polluted places. Plastic outdoor furniture melting in Hell. You're surrounded with smoke, some fire simulation set off by fuse-lit grenades. Oil smell in the night air. Your cornea. You get me back to the hotel. White shirt tight against my chest. President Ricky is on all fours, dumbfounded. He drinks Budweiser from a coffee cup. Blood trickles down the bathroom wall. I share a Budweiser with him. I smoke a cigarette out in the parking lot. I hail a taxicab. I snap at President Ricky. Rectify your mistakes I tell him. President Ricky is maligned. President Ricky is suspicious. He loves the badness. He plays different musical instruments to a packed auditorium. His hair slick with blood. President Ricky takes me out to an exotic club. We get private dances. I'm burnt up. You open your mouth. I wear men's shoes. Scrawny male shoes. Blood on your thighs. The sun comes out. I don't want to be buried alive. I apply my makeup. I'm becoming ordinary meat. Paste on my nose. Colour smeared on lips. I need to slow down. Stiff in further sexual advances. You wear a cloth nightgown. A cat meows. I stack cardboard boxes. Cool night air. Stimulants. Champagne. Muddy footmarks on the carpet. Photographs. Discharge from my mouth. My ear to the ground. Sinusoidal waves. Sound pressure. Loading dock. I lose my cool. Solar flares inside my brain. Possessed by an old gnome. There are people here. I close the door quietly. Moss and plaque and dry toothpaste. Blood samples spill into public baths. Great serpents with antennae and smallpox. The medical charts of rich alcoholics. Roadhouse beside a rural bordello. Police raid the boardroom. Bath soap used on body with a vengeance. A Midwest killer turns himself in for a medical operation. The portable x-ray machines are wheeled in. Smoke and combustible materials, chemical pellets. Surface smoke. Sub-machineguns on the streets of Garden City. Street value on the black market for stolen turbines. The soft flesh of the plastic cock. The erotic reality of horny billionaires. Blood congealing in the bathtub. Foam and cotton towels. A skeleton of bones, yellow spots on your skin. Water against the embankment. Tall crests. Robust undertow. Health department rejecting discourse and intellectual atmosphere. University President has light-headedness. Anthropologist with a restless mind drinking a bitter espresso. The steady flow of sugar upon the riverbed. Empty chairs at the adjacent table. A vacant seat at the student hangout. Primates take over San Diego. Gun dealers in Long Beach. You become a club promoter in San Francisco. Outdoor speakers at a press conference. Your Chevy Impala becomes a homeless shelter. Campfires attract coyotes and leave behind human bones. A wooden box with rotting bottles. President Ricky's mouth full of orange donuts. Enemy identified by soldiers produces murderous results. Mass murder makes newspaper headlines. President Ricky reads with interest and joy. President Ricky hides out in his wood cabin playing with his tape measure. A paper bag full of empty sequences. The murder rate in major cities such as El Paso. The air pollution in Linfen and Port-Au-Prince. A blacksmith working in a heartbreaking slum. Healthcare in the nastiest places in the Northern hemisphere is to be handled by a small gambling firm. President Ricky will oversee this operation. World poverty to be tackled with a dousing of weak sulfuric. Porn movies and the LA club scene. Cocktail waitresses wear stilettos. Plastic surgeons cruise strip clubs. The flashing lights of a patrol car. The black shoes of humanoids. The automatic timer of the ventilation fan. The barren hallway between the communication room and the conference room. Upper-level accountants in the dispatch office. A rocket launcher with surface-to-air missiles. A garbage bin against a brick wall. Fully-automatic weapons hidden in the pool halls of Huntington. Pistol ammunition for purchase in the factory outlet malls of Rockville Centre. Militant groups inhabit the manor homes of Massapequa. Denim jackets. Trolley cars pass at uncertain intervals. You breathe heavily. You scratch my body with your free hand. You kiss me again. The US military votes in a new leader. Dire warnings on LCD screens beside the FDR Drive off-ramp. Violence to my body. He cums before me. I'm too lazy to clean him off. I have no energy. I can't remember his name. Soft enchantments. You look at me embarrassed. You have blonde hair. You ejaculate twice. Cum over my chest. You land on the mattress after being fucked by me. Your arm is scabby. You ask me to massage your asshole. A woman sits and wipes her lips. You pull me between your legs. We're dressed in cardboard cutouts of ourselves. President Ricky's behind the shower screen. Limbs pressed against wet glass. Mud turtles boiled in their shell casing. Call girls with painted legs, perfumed thighs, moving, blooming, nails pierced, ripped skin. President Ricky has a sip from a bottle cap. Strawberry sauce slurped on my t-shirt. Antihypertensive medications wrapped in ripped stockings. The elevator doesn't work. Corroded metal over the stents. Arteries of an old man. Doctors investigate M.R. imaging. The computer screen secretes a gelatin coating. It is 2 degrees inside Bellevue. The heating is broken. The pores on your skin. The doctor's test the stent again. The Bellevue administrators call a press conference. I saw a replay of the press conference in Mexico City. You work at the anti-drug unit. You work out near Newark Airport. Automatic weapons in the Goodwill stores of Dix Hills. Contraband in the cow tunnels of the Lower West Side. 3.5 pounds of enriched uranium in a basement factory in Rochester. You have an American passport. A beam from a flashlight. You make your exit. You study me closely. My heart pounds. The suddenness of turning off a mental switch. Your cell phone rings. You are being watched. The nightlife of SOHO. It is close to midnight. A cry of pure tongue. You evade my direct answers. Your muscles protrude extraordinarily. SOHO is sleeping. Cash registers in your apartment. Dead people beneath construction sites. Celebrity interviews in a glossy book. The black stream of identical holograms. The hypnotic states of Lucifer. A copper box is now the bridal bed. Fresh blood on President Ricky's gory lips. His skin creeps from eternal rest. Transitory things evaporate upon hearing his firm voice. You hold out your hand to the neurologist. You are behind your desk reading industriously. You're in training for the New York Marathon. Social media in meltdown. A lean black man wearing a Soviet Army officer's cap. California has a peaceable nature. You need to fix past mistakes. A snowbound car with crystalline feathers in the trunk. Imprisonment in different part-time jobs. The shower curtain in your fingers. You've spent multiple lifetimes in your complete image. You wear black stockings. Nail polish spilt on your lace brassiere. You spend the summer months residing in official agencies that offer twenty-four-hour emergency services. A new Smartphone in your one-bedroom flat. Dead body which is a chalky colour. The skin hangs in deep shadows, black half-spheres. You move with instinct. Templates and instruction manuals for SMGs found in a toilet cubicle at Grand Central Station. A butcher knife leaning against war trophies. Crates of pepper spray and metal batons hidden in the deepest part of the Okefenokee. You design a safety mechanism for homemade pipe bombs. Steel slivers in the flesh of your palm. Smokeless powder on your tongue. Matchhead shavings that cause nausea. Piss stains on the wallpaper. Corn soup smells like hot sweat. Steam on the projection screens. Cryo-patients injected with plant spores. Gas bottles bobbing in the East River. Saudi Arabia moves to the Midwest. Standard images lit up by flashlight. Food eaten by homeless people. It is the right time for me to be sick. Your iris. Plastic box beneath the shower head. Copious amounts of alcohol. Burger King hands out balloons to its customers. Cab driver with small bills in rubber band. Carpet-bombing of Cambodia. Billboards advertising excursions to space colonies. Seroquel implanted in the embankments of Manhattan. My eyes are puffy. Medical instruments probe your right ventricle. A drowning at Niagara Falls. Plain sealed envelopes full of stolen cigarettes. Detective investigations into NYC Chief Medical Examiner. The penthouse terrace is filled with black wooden coffins. You write your name on an envelope. Camera pulls back. You write your telephone number on an envelope. We're in your bedroom. It is night. You're having a normal sleep. The phone booth inside the department store is demolished.

Satchels of strong coffee in your overnight bag. President Ricky advises me that small animals have a warm personality. Designer aphrodisiacs are given new expiration dates. It is the right time for President Ricky to be sick. Plastic box beneath the shower head. Copious amounts of drugs. Burger King hands out balloons to its customers. Cab driver rolls small bills in rubber band. Your limp cock in a leather mini-dress. Lipstick in your boxer shorts. Thick eyeglasses and a blonde wig. Overdone makeup. LSD and dieting. Pizza parlour has a takeaway option only. Underneath the night sky your body swings. I remove your wedding ring. Nerve gases provide temporary disorientation. Poison gas pumped into the Applebee's in White Plains. Bare breasts, panting against your skin. You stand there. Stirring the evening. Giant animals wander the streets. Your body jolts upon the mattress. Horrible things happening to you. Your pale eyelids. Your eyeballs as black orbs. Fingertips grip the balustrade. Confused memory approaches me. Memory fades. Blue eyes in a breathless body. The dark evening. Hurricane winds. Engines up on cinder blocks. Motor oil on the hotel carpet. Television on. Plastic outdoor furniture in the kitchen. Sun-warped. Cracking. Peeling. You're not seeking any publicity. UFOs now classified as 'religious weapons.' You sleep wrapped in influential newspapers. Weekend parties with packages of LSD. Shoe leather in your mouth. Asleep in the Gramercy Park Hotel. Asteroid belts and complex organisms. Medical researchers whose blood drizzles. Slaves with shrewd eyes. Deer-like creatures in the shadows. Unwary beasts in protective suits. Tequila inserted into apple pie. DA diagnosed with Septic Peritonitis. The Missing Persons Clearinghouse has a fleet of squad cars provided by Chrysler. Groceries from the Wholefoods at Union Square don't come with any written guarantees. Your shoes and hosiery are trucked in from Cincinnati. You head over to the payphone and pick up the receiver. A warm summer afternoon. The cocaine is mislaid, overlooked. A widower with his shirt wide open. Buttons pop everywhere. You laugh anyway. Transplants and antibodies in cargo holds bound for North Africa. I look over my shoulder. Nothing behind me. I have a spare key. I guess I could stay at the hotel. You look at me. My right leg is missing. You attach my leg. Your ciliary lens. I hurry to the elevator. You run a small gambling firm from your apartment. Weak sulfuric smell from construction sites. Locusts around rubbish bins. Cash registers buried with dead people. The wristwatch ticks on the faceless patient. Non-native species discovered in the Soviet Union. Your curiosity with shirt and shoes only shows a short-term interest. Celebrity interviews collected in a glossy book. A black stream of identical holograms. The hypnotic states of Lucifer together in a copper box. Your bridal bed covered in fresh blood. My skin creeps over your gory lips. Your black teeth. President Ricky restrains you to the floor. Sweat forms on your skin. President Ricky gets alcohol delivered to your tent. He implores you to take a sip. Xanax-flavoured. Brown eggnog. President Ricky presses strange devices against your sternum. Plastic bag full of makeup. President Ricky takes you on a boat cruise. Gossip magazines. A certain lassitude within Hollywood. Murmur in your veins. Drunk falling down. President Ricky massages your mossy temples. The eternal rest of transitory things. Small animals with awful hunger. Spit in a foam cup at the police station. Doors squeak. Film projector pitching images of black eyes onto Astor Row sidewalk. City streets as empty prisms. Telephone sits in a small corner outlet. White wires seared through. Umbilical cords around stiffened fingers. You look across the Port Authority Bus Terminal. Nothing but a homeless person on a bus to Queens. Total warmth in my y-fronts. Sensitive lips on your body's curves. Aroused by your blue eyes. Your red lips are friendly. I laugh at how cock-hungry I am. Sexual fantasies. Undergarments mass-produced from pure wool fabrics. Super-fine shirts that are made-to-measure from 25c per shirt. The curtains. A kicking light rushes in. The tiny windowpane. Blood all over the floor. Loose footings. Police cars. A giant slug. Flames swinging above your skull. Underwear in pencil skirts. DMT during lunchtime. Toxic lungs inside the prayer room. I reach the barricade. Police lashing bodies. An encyclopedia of knots. IBM super-computer in your basement. Gene therapy with your mistress. Physical acts in unsafe structures. You're a full-blown masochist. S/M in the piss-smeared nights. Recreational therapy with stimulating images. Letters to the editor. Photos on an adult online magazine. President Ricky with a perpetual diseased liver. Sweat pores in Astoria. New dimensions to the apocalypse. Silver coins in exchange for superfoods. Stock prices collapse. Babysitter kills toddler. A private hospital wraps lifeless torsos in rubber blankets. You load, fire, and reload your shotgun. Religious service on the street. I stumble on the stairs. Police cars come to a halt. The winding hallway. Water in the basin. You're swathed in white silk cloth. You play with a length of rope. Pasta bubbles in soapy hot water. Your skeletal frame. There's something not right with you. You're on the bedspread. I'm in the bath. You've decorated the bathroom. It smells like shit. Foodstuffs and amphetamines. Simulation of the new sun. President Ricky ejaculates in his underpants. President Ricky pisses on my leg. I step in front of the sliding door. Blindfolds of electricity spark in sucking, lurking emulsions of room. This world will crash. Swing door into the kitchen. An anatomy school without subjects. Newspaper reporters carry Samsonite suitcases in their unclean hands. Your vital organs are eviscerated by a skilled surgeon. My physician went to the Harvard Medical School. She repays her student financial aid via monthly payments. I spend my days examining people who have the smallest veins in the world. My office is near the toilet block. You like to roam the toilet block, looking for sex. I enter the toilet block. You demand oral sex. My heart rate is placed under investigation. You experience no obvious injury. You watch some old erotic movie that is projected onto your apartment wall. You hear the beating of hands on your door. A handgun discharges. Someone hits the ground. Bubble bath and liquid teeth. Your middle finger outlining pungent scent on President Ricky's skin. President Ricky ejaculates and rides the adrenalin rush. Demise of his pretty face. Pointy toe in his mouth. The unpleasant taste of condoms and cigarette puffs.

Sex acts that cause salmonella poisoning. President Ricky refers to the woman's mouth as a worthless piece of voice murmuring. A young doctor with his head downward. Your shiny shoes in a steamy bath. Dirty hands for body inspection. The subcutaneous tissue on your wide lips. Plasma leakage from right nipple. American planes over President Ricky's apartment. President Ricky has a cardiovascular collapse. You purchase a semi-porcelain dinner set for a sale price at a home furnishings store on Broadway. In your personal lifestyle you play the perfect victim. You are no backward killer. Long swallows of semen in cheap hotel. The warm trail of an uncomfortable burn. The pleasure of burning yourself. Your thoughts float. The male reproductive organ. Thumbs inside spines. Eyes within placenta. Insects served during dinner service. Rain encircles Brooklyn Bridge. Soiled beds. Stairwells. Night. Dissolve to: Hotel rooms. Patios. Bed sheets. Brown paper. Hotel staff. Back massage on East 14th Street. Snarling underage guy. Woolen gloves in coat pocket. Metal smells. You purchase roll-on deodorant from the convenience store. Thighs filled with synthetic water. NYC on a projection screen. Sunlight on female teeth. Bedside lamplights. Palm around my throat. I look back. The TV is on. News reports. The total sea inside me. Lightning frames the windows. Oil on the woodwork. The news report voice. The news reporter pointing, hollering, working closely with the CIA. I take my coat off. A teen party for freaks with malignant diseases. Pizza delivery cancelled throughout Manhattan. Death certificates issued automatically. NYC as post-industrial war-zone. Psychotic children with deep anxiety. Gas station robberies and movie theatres with a violent language. America in slow motion. Your minimum wage job. McDonalds throughout Mexico. Tent cities in a recession economy. Financial blowout causes extreme blood pressure. Resistant bacteria in your Gucci loafers. Parasites in your cigarettes. A heavy smoker with sunburn. Extracts from citrus trees causing defective skin pigmentation. Tooth decay as a birthmark. Expensive gambling in Israel. Cigarettes from my trouser pocket. My photo ID. A face imprinted in blood and the world. You're asleep. Further news is relayed to me by radio. Embers over your whole body. Knuckles of sudden fear. You're on your last legs. You feel slight, bony, like a sunken sea vessel. I defend myself. I stand up. Further developments. Brutal interrogations. I pull your cock harder. An hour later, we're having dinner. Dead boy on the Upper West Side. The radar operator, inside the penthouse, works at the end of a long corridor. You wear white trousers and take strange drugs. You make animal gestures in the stairwell at night. The hotel manager takes a deep breath. A death rattle beneath his fur cap. All bodies in the residential suburbs divide into pulsations and shapeless emotions. Metabolic disturbances inside the hardware store. President Ricky is average height, and he has fine features. He has tiny breasts and thick brown hair. He has almond eyes and a firm mouth. Warm laughter over his red lips. High heels in the empty corridor. They move in an uneven rhythm. President Ricky talks with a disinterested voice. Elevator man's face in the small mirror. Your insides churn. Side streets. A man sits in a dim stairwell. Loud silence. A national emergency, a nuclear meltdown at the Indian Point Energy Centre. My throat tingles. Hot saliva. Telephone call. Sample video files containing nudes and telephone numbers. You bookmark your favourite online adult magazines. Sexy centerfolds from Chernobyl and other polluted places. Plastic outdoor furniture ordered from Indianapolis. Campfires surrounded by coyotes. Human bones discovered in a wooden box. Rotten bottles hold orange donuts. The bleeding mouth of my enemy has been identified. Soldiers detail their murderous results. Newspaper headlines plaster your wood cabin. Tape measure inside a paper bag. The narcotics market in El Paso. The murder rates of major cities. Coal towns of Soleil. The air pollution in Port-Au-Prince. Haiti. Your left shoulder under hot water, heavy heat. You're employed to gain profitable turnarounds for potential investment opportunities. You're drafting proposals for a promising gas pipeline that needs research capital. Certain motels out on Long Island. Comfortable pillows in our room. Sears catalogue on the magazine rack. We make out. We giggle. You finish with another boy. A burning within you. You suck cum off me. I lead you down the street. You open a water bottle. You pour the water into my mouth. You lift my skirt from behind. I lean and turn around. You step back. You're toned. You have a well-muscled body. You find your way deep inside me. You wear silver high heels. You stumble closer to the soft tip of my curves. You remove my clothes. Your thumb and forefinger in my ass. You find both of these prospects uninspiring and a dead end. Small blood vessels smoked in carbon dioxide. Your esophagus filled with stomach acid. Bikini briefs beneath your nylon jacket. Your sequin breast. Gasoline savings in the latest Chrysler. Laboratory tests for hair shampoo. Soppy lather on your toothbrush. Skin disease and heartburn. Adhesive tape on your hypodermic injections. Press releases for illegal sound. Major oil companies with seasonal layoffs. Accident investigation with no gimmicks, no charge, immediate delivery. Easy monthly payments and wholesale discount prices. Electronic equipment for cancer treatments shipped to England. You fuck biker guys on leather seats for the lewd sensation. You lodge your female cousin into a luxury retirement home because she has a terminal disease. Body fluids dispensed by military personnel. Common slogans used to advertise new social drug. Long-term consumption of the industrial system causes psychosis. President Ricky is an inoffensive person with an enormous paunch. Immigration authorities conduct espionage and check pass port stamps. The linguistic inability of your full-length mouth. Space navigation through three-dimensional waves by light aircraft. Genitals with price tags. Kidneys inside skulls. Elbows constructed out of shins. Forearms growing from necks. Your throat gurgles with psychic bruises. Fluid imbalances within the populace create an endemic of physiological shock. Military base stores receptacles of liquid plasma. You study the sexual neuroses of wealthy young men from Rochester. Radar screen installed inside a storm drain. Sewerage delivered to refugee compounds.

Makeshift cities to offer sex change surgery. Wall Street starts investing in ice boxes. Dishwasher gloves on top of radio speakers. Luncheon service that consists of cobwebs and artificial grass. Your earlobe. Cocaine rubbed into the ear canals. Television, post-midnight in the late 1980s, was all Evangelical Christianity, and advertisements for herpes medication. Game show contestants turning up on news reports. Studio lights on the television screen. Flavoured body dressed in Buddhist robes. Black patent leather shoes give agency to mass aneurisms. You formulate statistical reports on pagan gods, race conflicts and routine insults that are common to industrial society. My organs shut down. Your hands edge over my body. Your cool grip upon my limbs. You wrap me in a big towel. My spider legs. Your open mouth swoops. Blood packages stolen from Manhattan Ear, Eye & Throat Hospital. Asleep in a Queens courtyard. Cough drops on the bedside table. Fresh towels over your translucent skin and ash-blonde curls. An outside call from the center desk put through to the rest room. You're in your business office. Display lights in the anteroom. Underage guy in the office cubicle. War gases and napalm attack. Your mouth on my abdomen. A total abandon to fever orgasms and spiritual exercises. Nervous agitation in the warm night. The therapeutic effects of a mild analgesic. A small daily dosage. Backpack on a park bench. A pathetic group of orphans and outcasts. You are homeless. Your parents are dead. You blush and turn your eyes to me. You enter your apartment at four o'clock. You knock on the door of the living room. You hear sobbing. Object meeting bare flesh.

My face flushes. My eyes are wide. You punish me for impertinence. Your figure is magnificent. Sculptured thighs. Skin is pale white. Extremely sensitive. The leather strap is short and thin. Swift, stinging strokes. Lip gloss on biceps. Polaroid sunglasses and secondhand watches. Jewelry and radios in your water closet. Stereo sets and cookware in your wardrobe. Silverware and hunting equipment under your bed. Glassware and linens in a suitcase. Drapery and fabrics on the furniture. Toys and fur stoles in the laundry. Trains in the rail yard. Blood in your Pepsi-Cola. War Department sets up at Grand Central Station. Microscopic films that detail interplanetary space. Future civilization guarantees future warfare. Hosiery and assorted clothing in the shower stall. Shoes in their shoe boxes. You fuck in the empty countryside. The CEO of a major oil company constructs steel-like muscles. He craves lifeguard shoulders and athletic legs. Office workers on 32nd Street drink synthetic beer. Dollar bills in plastic containers. Airplane trips over the Atlantic. Homeless students in Portugal. Deep leather around forehead and hair. Crossword puzzles in The New York Times. You collect rubber ducks and manuscripts of aborted literature. Police paranoia about the formation of a hippy stronghold in Massapequa. Your small red eyes. You remove my clothes. You take money for sex. You push my lips. You suck the slime. Long penis beneath miniskirt. Long orgasms. You take pictures. A bottle of whiskey. You breath hard. You feed me toast. Urine in ass. Whole tongue in ass. You pull me backwards. I have to kiss you. You open your mouth first. Your tongue between my legs. Precious stones and greenish coils inside your blunt nose. Reddish-brown fins on the back of your hand. The amazing speed of your grotesque wings. The amazing speed of your imminent car crash. Reflective lenses in your eye sockets. Retractable razor blades in your fingers. Lice in hairpieces. The phosphoresce of your breasts, bicep, long black hair, right hand, left arm and cock. We're fucking. The warm vapours of your wide lips. Great fissures in North America and Mogadishu. Shoe fetishism catches on in London. Horse eyes. Magical space. Pussy. Weird shit. Total bullshit. There are now general strikes in England and Russia. You write exclusive reports regarding fascist alliances with trade-union leaders. You present exhibitions on behalf of the armament industry to peacetime governments. I note your terrible ears and dark eyes, and that black stuff you call your stiff hair. Your eardrum. A circular section cut into the soil at Pelham Park Bay. A mystery construction made of white fibres and fabric. Religious beings in tweed coats talking to television audiences. Animal skins cured by tobacco smoke. Viral diseases behind fly screen windows. Prison riot subdued by blowgun darts. Potent neurotoxins implanted into assassination devices. A police officer slaps my body on the table. I swallow your cock. You smile. A message on the TV. You pin your lips to my ass. Patients wait for the doctor. You gasp. You rub your nipples on my body. You pound my ass. I can't walk. You are close enough. You step into the doorway. You masturbate. You stand in the rain. You sit back on your heels. The court pathologist mentioned that your next door neighbour had disposed of his children's nanny the night before. He'd forced a firearm into her mouth. We make out on the couch. We're lying on top of a Sears catalogue. You giggle. Florida destroys all its fireproof buildings. Silicone materials are replaced with champagne. Local boy's cock inside filthy holes. President Ricky zeroes in on the local language. A wet massage that is throbbing and half-aroused. Cocaine on your bath towel. Puerto Rico is relocated to the Pacific Ocean. Heavy luggage on a bathroom scale. Laundry starch like light sandpaper. Your car furnished and expenses paid. Face surgery after accident investigation. Naked CEO fucks senior citizen. Earthquake in the Gobi Desert. Plus-sized package with correct postage. Cartoons with Infographics. Standardized exams for sexual research. Death medicine for monthly repayments. Junk food for Africa. You feel naughty as you finish off another boy. A burning within you. The boy sucks some cum off your waist. You lead me down the street. I am done. You open a water bottle and pour the inside into my mouth. It is cold. You lift my skirt from behind. You see me as you wish to see me. You lean into me and then turn me around. You step back. You are toned. You have a well-muscled body. I wear silver high-heels. You stumble closer to the soft tip of my curves. Erect nipples and misshapen head. Intricate cogs beneath the main control lever turn. Red sunlight through the blinds. You take a deep breath and mention astronomical physics. You discuss your utter dejection with stupid movies. Handgrips on tobacco pipes. Official checkpoints for paramilitary weapons. The restless moats of Wards Island. Strange creatures of solid flesh flay in the

Bronx Kill. Departed bodies in knotted grass. Strong drugs produce psychosomatic froth. Wind blows burlap around the alleys of Jerusalem. You're in a pencil skirt conducting ESP experiments. Sun pours producing wide streaks. Slight movement on the prairies. Your metallic cigarette case in a dumpster. Your hand plunges for a cigarette. You work the nightshift on a shit job. Illegal imprisonment in an old phone booth. Technical analysis of your morning cough. I glance back at the lights of the Bronx, loud music, young teens. Velvet wallpaper. Tissue paper. Anonymous person on the slick floor of your kitchen. Unbearable loneliness. Wooden door to a small den. Fresh linen. A television screen. A clothes basket with a blanket inside. A man's voice. Evacuation warnings. A small stove top in your tenement. House phone not working. I don't need dinner. A journalist's voice on the television set. Experts making assertions. Your books, your fashion magazines all in the doorway. Bed sheets clean wet cock. Condoms in coat pocket. Political images in subway parks. You kiss his ribcage. Action involves ass. You rub cum together with antifreeze. You attack me with a disturbing hostility. Disciplinary action taken by your employer, not the police. There is no need for this. Rubbish piled up outside the Park Avenue Armoury. I drink while working. Track suits with brand names. Photographs out of focus. You detail in a notebook that you have greater sexual attraction to Greeks and Spaniards. You also advise that you have a congenital predisposition to latex. Trench knives and brass knuckles. Bayonets and sawed-off shotguns. Metal tubes and pocket clips. Teargas cartridges and radio antennae. Crude mechanisms with coil springs. Elastic bands holding pistol grips together. Metal tubes. Pipe fittings. Automatic pistols with violent recoils. Your substance intake. Homosexual publications discuss drug addictions. Hollywood celebrities in Norway. Cigarettes in the computer library. Intelligent life inside a cloud mass. Red dots on a long slope. Sensitive mortals with abrupt impatience. Loose sleeves on your old sweater. This hot planet with its acid tongue. Your pale eyes looking over a tundra of small rodents. The greenish iridescence of your huge eyes. Your brain records reconnaissance methods and the wire enclosures of NYC. Giant men wander carrying laser guns. Hurricanes hover throughout the dark evening. You grab my shoulder. I breathe hard. Chill inside the bathroom. You push your cock inside me. Engine up on cinder blocks. Motor oil smeared on television screen. Liquor in your gut. You speak. You won't let me speak. People drown. People rest in cabs. Music in the hallway. You run to catch the bus. You ask to be buried alive. The sea is wild. Your eyeballs full of answers. Pharmacy catalogues on the backseat of the bus. This is a lie. Smoke. Fires smolder. Telephone conversations. I run to your apartment. You're speeding without the headlights on. Money kept in a rusted bread tin. Hidden supermarkets. I skateboard. Broken pylons. Advanced kinds of NYC. The bus is packed. I don't want to go to work. Subtitles beneath the pages of this book. Fashion models amass in the member's area. Security guards wearing women's shoes. BDSM advertised on cigarette packets. Clear cold windless afternoons. Weed packages and wine barrels carried in rubbish bins. You're on the ocean. The migration of prehistoric man along great rivers. Land-bearing giants stomp out campfires and gorge on frogs. Light switch broken in your apartment block. You caught Hepatitis C from a ballpoint pen. Anarchic death-state in suburban homes. Car keys and cell phone. Trigger fingers and prosthetic eyeballs. Your fingertip attachments constructed with pewter castings. Flesh-binding powder upon your skin. Caustic substances that cause permanent blindness. Hollow tubes and open pouches containing aerosol canisters. Your erotic manner provides us with mutual gratification. I don't know much. Underwear inside my suitcase. Icy background of the East River. Your money purse left in the lobby of the Woolworth Building. You hair wash on a daily basis. You wish to live a normal life. Your toe nails clipped and polished. You post a selfie on Instagram. Text messages to next door neighbour. A blonde man with shaved pubic hair. His muscular coarseness. You wash his body. His body jolts. His chest cavity heaves. His dead skin. The blonde man sits unaware. I turn the main kitchen lights off. Listed tears. Your clothes taken off, your actions recorded amongst sweat, steam and water pressure overhead. Descriptions on websites about fungi and bacteria are an infantile attempt to get you to laugh. The marsh and cemetery of Washington Square Park. You turn the water taps on. You wield your hips over me. An awful winter season runs through the French Embassy on Fifth Avenue. No television. Strawberries wrapped in copies of the New

York Post. Bruises under your straw hair. Noise. Chiming carousels. Hips. Scabs. Scratches. Close-up of your sharp nose. Black forms fondle galactic microforms. Mountain range in the rear-view mirror. Alien air minus gravity. Earth oxygen encrusts smooth, worn boulders. Strange clouds seen through your field glasses. Wide panoramas of featureless cylinders. Air currents and thermal chimneys. Strange invasion of telescopic eyes. Toilet stops. The dancefloor. Amyl nitrate. Nose jammed with muck. Tobacco smoke crosses over your lips. You're considerably figurine. Future people. Secret catches of sleep. You're on the bed. The bed opens. Your form repulses me. Your face light and dry. I am desperate. Press releases coming in the mailbox. A vacant jilt in the layers of air. Gravestones. Gin-drenched. Gimlet-eyed. Beautiful boys. This isn't the penthouse floor. You're under the bedsheets. Manicurist in pale suit, new tie, smoking fat cigars. Children scream. New card tricks. Champagne dinners. Tramping in heavy snow. Rain on pharmacy catalogues. Your mouth glistens in the mirror. A noose at Fraunces Tavern. A sharp knife wrapped in brown paper. Wet body in a photographic booth. Limbs starve with tobacco smoke. A flea-bitten saline bag propped on an IV pole. Interrogation doctrines coming through via telephone lines. Milk carton on a large wooden table. The square windows of your apartment. A professional finish on the floorboards. A burgundy pattern on an oriental rug. My entire torso burns. Your hips scream. My muscles cry. Your footsteps echo inside a vacant building. Your apartment building in uptown nighttime stillness. Empty streets.

Movie's projected onto the walls of St. Bartholomew's Church. A severed right arm found in Ryders Alley. Upon hearing this news, you take out life insurance, a three million dollar policy on yourself. You photograph a strange man who wears only a black thong. Bodies on a packed bus. Towering creatures. You pat my leg. You swaddle me within computer systems. A length of cord around my wrist. Body unbalanced. In the crematorium I wear a striped suit jacket and denim jeans. Religious fervor and incense smoke. Your body, stiff and drunken. Foam from your mouth. I hold a tropical plant I found at the rubbish tip. Candles inside railway carriages. Trains in the Hudson Yards. Blood washes upon Grand Central Station. Sulfuric acid on Adidas shell toes. Plutonium dust on decomposing body. Anthrax spores on the street signs lining Wooster Place. You experience psychotic symptoms in Laos. Skin opening and delivering blood. Wind tunnel and electricity pole. Birthday cards from overseas soldiers. Main street during the watery night. You're arrested on a second-degree theft charge. ESP. Tight shot. Close up. Mug shot. The nervous system of rioters. Cocaine deals leave you laughing. Coarse language. Miniature knives and thumb daggers hidden in Duffy Square. Rodent-like forms and insect creatures. Primitive worlds with superior races. Alien minds with upper-level evolutionary sequences. Blunt fingers on your right hand. Sea levels and open mouths. Cold nerves inside time travel. Red curls over shoulders. Green eyes analyzed by language enthusiasts. Intricate equipment engenders field reports. Busy machine-world. You advise me that I lack intellectual consistency. Dead stars made from mucous membrane. Erogenous zones for people underweight. Corporal penances for ardent sluts. Civilizations of pederasts fuck with feverish activity. Transparent bubbles full of pale parasites. Multiple punctures in plastic surgery. Hard surfaces display novelty items like toy handguns and x-ray specs. Black market dealers selling long batons, aluminum rods and metal knuckles. Strangling of vicious dogs on Washington Street. Nerve endings shrouded and coated in mucous membranes and painful welts. Barometric pressure beneath Seminary Row. Unconscious assailant buried beneath cinderblocks. Pulmonary artery torn apart on St Nicholas Avenue. Sun shower on the Shinran Statue. Wetness. It's daytime and you're in the kitchen. You separate your tablets and vitamins into their daily dosages. A Jehovah Witness knocks on your backdoor. You offer him a molasses-type of drink. Dominant lesbians haunt the streets of Morningside Heights. They let me above the lobby in the Webster Apartments. The evening crumbles. Empty subway stations. A motionless door. The hallways hum. Damp summer air upon yellow taxis. Filthy hands on dry leaves. Your body shifts on the mattress. Your body sweats on the brocade sofa. Motorcycle oil on my bedspread. Your rheumy eyes. NYPD states that the crash victim was dragged into a ditch and then sexually assaulted. A fateful morning. More murder in Sheep Meadow. A doorman laid out, lifeless on the vast lawn. Chain-smoking in Stuy Town. Chronic damage to large arteries causes valvular dysfunction. Aneurismal swelling beneath an opaque membrane. You eat me out eagerly. You're inside my vagina. You pull your mouth out. You remove my clothes. You insert a thumb and forefinger. You taste the wetness of my breast. A strange man watches on. You never take money for sex. A soaked pussy. You lick me clean. I clutch your long penis. You put your fists through the glass pane. I stand there. Your knuckles exposed. You hurry to the street. A limited range of feelings. My sleep disturbance. Your social isolation. My withdrawal into the apartment. Insecticides. I worked to purchase new clothes. Sauerkraut heaped on your hot dog. You draw on your cigarette. You look behind you. Your eyes roll. We sit around in wheelchairs, smoking and chatting to each other. Human worshippers. Four hours pass. We have an intermission. You take off your belt. You look at me. A rimy tear on my fingertip. Music from down the hall. Taxis running tourists all over Manhattan. Wet airports. Parasitic specimens falling over in sober elegance. Fat cheeks on unhealthy children. Small sums of evolutionary movement. Water hidden behind your bread tin. You upturn a pair of slippers and inspect them. Chair upholstered in sweat. The oft-distorted Atlantic Ocean. A tight spiral of steady whirlwinds. Air currents clockwise spiral. Peculiar clouds seep into the control panel. Chemical affinities scar your long fingers. Neat moustache hides your sour personality. Sea levels and nose bleeds. All average citizens garnished with oxygen masks. You wear triangulation glasses. A yellow dot on space charts. My skin is waterlogged. Saline in the veins. It is just after midday. You extract my body from the hallway. I crawl into the bathroom. Nerve gases.

The dusk light over New Jersey. A plastic bag of gloomy diagnosis and drugs. The yellowish colour of bony matter discarded on Lenox Avenue. Wicker picnic baskets burning in the vast expanse of Hudson River Park. Shopkeepers draw on lottery tickets. Jam lids and butter tins scattered throughout. Riverside Park. Soap dishes in Chinatown. Inky paintings distributed by the War Departments. A slight breeze through Central Park. The unimaginable heat of Manhattan. A rusty sky over the East River. You throw Beaujolais to put the flames out. Knickers rubbed in salt spray and stained with grass smudges. You make out with a subordinate, until you realize you're sitting on a stack of Sears catalogues. Proposition for life. You experience a stricken feeling after eating a tea biscuit. You sketch outlines of Rita Ora on small white cards. You were once a blonde receptionist. Your employer put you in precarious sexual conditions. An entire life before your eyes. Evening. Your gloved hands throughout a harsh winter. Your eyes flicker. The American public hidden underneath a small trapdoor. Tire jack in a square manhole. Car polish on the spare windscreen. The crisp skin of scorched lovers. A man in a straightjacket. A flame lights him up. A vase of flowers. An interactive display of plywood trees and inferior genes. The empty space of cobalt bodies. Your black eyes. Tree leaves in Autumn. Swivel chair at the secretarial desk. Identification cells during phone sex. I lower my head. President Ricky wears a fur coat. It rustles without the aid of wind. I light a cigarette. Eroded membranes like fabric samples. Semen in President Ricky's crotch. I rush into the courtyard. You fall on the bed. You kick the nightstand away. Are you cattle? Shoe leather fills your nostrils. Poor folk in the railway warehouses. Steel foundries of physical pleasure. You were someone's husband once. Blood drizzles from a wound. Angular fingers on your breasts. Hands inside a wet crevice. The clinical practices of depressive illnesses. Everyday violence caught on video tape. Tourists trapped in taxis. Transplant organs hidden inside a bus door in Bangkok. Temporary coffins at the employment bureau. Medical students sequestered to Oklahoma Penitentiary. Gunman hiding in the torture house. Secret code provided to police officials. Photographs for 30 cents. Seven men dying is seen as an evil omen. Walking around Potter's Field the entire night. A card table and chair. An open roof under stars. Rosy skies over wooden coffins. The inmate's hand is a different size than mine. You're watching the weather channel. A golden sun above glaciers. Dark forests on the Himalayas. Andes full of ice field ranges. Unbreathable air discloses whimsical dialogue. Efficient patterns engraved upon impressive terrain. The Chief Zoologist fucks the Radiation Specialist. Time Machines for sale on West 45th Street. The Vietnam War fought between Russia and Korea. Free brochure advertising glamour photography. Radiator pumps imported from Mexico. Exotic girls with blood red hands. Children as drug addicts. Metallic smoke hazes. NYPD states that a missing Queens women was found dead in her car. She had holes in her head. A faraway apparition of mouths. Desperate breathing in hotel bathrooms, orgasms, crotch, ass and cocaine. Your prettiest teeth in another girl's tight mouth. You like to fuck in basketball shorts. Pericardium excised from the dead bodies on Great Jones Street. Internal parts. Whole coagulum and red globules on your shirt collar. Late-teen mouth around cock. You photograph this, then submit to a wet skirt, a gentle squeeze on my pussy. Storage costs for frozen human heads. Mime enthusiasts. Age of a boy. The height of a boy. Techno-erotic paganism in the nightlife of Shanghai. Straightforward updates on the progress of the BM&F Bovespa via hypertext and computer graphics. Fiber optic links through the autonomous zones of a thawing Arctic. Artificial life. Cocks and fucks in the center of NYC. The yellow colour and pulpy matter on your underwear. Common pus secreting from a muscular substance. The gangrene adhesions on lifeless physiques. Bogus doctor. Wet clit on an evil guy. Sparse hairs in my mouth during blow job. Slow motion of limbs during rheumatic fever. You kiss bony heads. A 12 pack of Michelob Ultra. Two quarts of creaming soda. You don't recognize me. You weigh me. You make me sign some paperwork. You hand me an information brochure to read at home. You rub a hideous grey salve on my forehead. Donated blood kept in milk bottles. Weight-loss clinics offering plastic surgery as consolation prizes. You sign documents using your formal name. You educate yourself on how to prevent an abdominal aortic aneurysm. You investigate the symptoms, diagnosis and treatments for lumbar spinal stenosis. The wetness of backyard sex practices. Rain across the baseball fields. Your car at the front entrance. A hellish swarm of beetle kings cover the tourist bus. Lips as fossils. The strident sounds of disintegrating subways. Purchasing Burger King for a five-year vacation. Food supplies are non-food, drowning in low tide, snorkeling in the cargo bay, work ID card pinned to back wall. Penthouse floor covered in trench coats. Yellow teeth caused by excessive liquor. Loaded gun discovered in the ballpark. Shrunken heads uncovered in Manchuria. Loaded gun pointed at the magazine photographer. Strange girls in the theatre foyer. Press agents conducting radio interviews. Fan magazines full of celebrity pictures. You're a lifelong bachelor. Loaded gun in your slender palm. Fingers bent backwards. Desert sands of Arizona. Cactus over the flat landscape. Elderly man with neat curves. The morbid obsession of your natural climax. Your supple feet in green heels. The dirty underlinen of Kendall Jenner. Dead faces disturb the sea captain. Black perforated scabs. The skull still hairless. In a business-like fashion to press the speaker button. I have a complete disinterest in your sex storm. Ass on feedback loop. Your apartment is a blank paradise. I smell of inexpensive perfume. I wear hosiery and super-fine shirts. They're made-to-measure. They cost 25 cents. Lacerated torsos transported to a private hospital. They're wrapped in rubber blankets. Newspaper reporters arrive. They have unclean hands. They wash them. Your vital organs are contained in suitcase. You're injected with government-issue chemicals to stop the auditory hallucinations. You're asked for your phone number. You hand over your credit card and driver's license. You attend morning mass, but read a comic book for the duration. You breathe the toxins from ghoul's mouth. The warm thrust of skin beneath silk blouse. You photograph a miracle girl who can fit an entire melon slice into her mouth. Giant machinery on Roosevelt Island generate vast public spectacles, sonic booms and explosions. Big toe, other human limbs use for medical science floating in the Gowanus Canal. Cryonics experts having their Christmas Party at the Coney Island Circus Sideshow. Family pet constructed in laboratory. Tumors caused by rectum malformation. Your diseased appearances and urethra abscesses. Secret experiments led by anti-hydergine extremists in the top floor of the Audubon Terrace. October assassination attempts in Green-Wood Cemetery. I'm wearing loose clothing and you can see my stretch marks. A massage with moisturizing cream. Young man keeps his tassel loafers in a small black box. Stasis effect among people in the street. Campfires inside Dakar. Adhesive cream paste on the African coast. Razor blades throughout 11th Street. Free samples of taxidermy. They are grotesque figures. Dead men scooped from the mournful sea. Salesman selling wallpaper from suitcases. You have nothing to worry about. You use to be selfish. We met inside the CVS one afternoon. I told you I had to meet up with my parole officer. Later I told you it was with my counselor. I set up an altar in your apartment. I never told you what the altar worshipped. I put five dollars down on the kitchenette. Your apartment was now lit with black candles. Long underwear held together with Scotch tape. A car door slams. Your body. I hear the sea. Sooty tobacco. Brine. Camera in my hand. The wind. Icicles. Your cellphone.

Outside the supermarket. You've got sinus trouble. You give your room key to me. I head to the liquor store. I leave by the side door liquor store. Conman performs nasty tricks. All sweet talk. High class businessman getting fucked in hotel room disposes of his professional reputation. Diamond ring glints in rainy night. Chicago collapses into black mountains. Food to offset your hangover. Paraffin wax burns in a tin lid. I let out a sigh. Jacket and cap on. The lower floor of the carpark. You're barefoot. You sip from your coffee that's on the nightstand. You're enjoying the drug. Our friends are waiting for us in the lobby. I could do with less surprise. Poppers from sex shops. You practice epileptic tremors. Knotted days of the ebony sun. Vapors in the bone of my sternum. You wrap me in fine hair. I buy some cigarettes. Bible knowledge about the existence of another Earth. Bird refuge on the islands of Indonesia. Bright brochures with full-colour photos left behind in a briefcase. General lawlessness from absolute monsters. You undergo elegant improvements to your body, skin components, mega-scale engineering for artificial body parts, new mandibles and pelvis ordered and fitted in time for Thanksgiving. The galloping building structures of Midtown Manhattan. Spermatic chord restructured into hair and teeth. Gastric juice interleaved into small-pox pustules. The long-term financial security of the modern world is a cultural myth. Human enterprise collapses. International charity agencies offer financial assistance to welfare moms on the 24th floor of the Empire State Building. Your blue pant leg in a photographic booth on Fort

Washington Avenue. Wet body and limbs starve. Stress remedies detailed in secret instructional booklet. Dollar bills bluster across 89th Street. People in the end stages of their life. You read an apologia regarding irrational reluctance to control worldwide environmental damage. The manuscript for this apologia is pasted behind the blue and gold-leaf zodiac mural that is on the ceiling of the Grand Central Station. Arithmetic scribbled into a notebook. Theoretical physics. Medical specialists. Clergymen in control of sewage-disposal systems. My financial backer on the telepathic screen wearing a rubbish medallion. B-grade movie from the late 60s conversing on LSD. Tobacco smoking while wearing leather electronics. Monster slugs wrapped in fur coats. Numerous tiny rodents rolling in the red grass. Sweat forms on the luminous trees. The painful moments during your EEG test. Brain implants delivered in woolen shawls. Your burgundy moustache and bare breasts. Shell-clad monsters roaming within the hurricanes. Hair garments draped over the dildo machine. Unusual men performing sports entertainment and sexual acts. New food sources from rotten produce. Birth-control plans for first world countries. Government bureaus firebombed by Siberian tribesman. Dry lips in the Gobi Desert. Mutinies in the industrial centers. Circuits malfunction on the JUQUEEN. The Deputy Sheriff commits suicide insider the jewelry store. It ruins his professional reputation. President Ricky wears a diamond ring. His hair is combed into angular fragments. He carries a read-only memory chip in his carryall. He wears cosmetics made from black rock formations. The exquisite pleasures from his home planet. Vast plains of beasts and unimportant appendages. The sexual impulse of neurotic subjects. President Ricky demands adequate gratification. Yellow water in parallel rivers. President Ricky dines with transvestites. Criminal gangs read comic books in psychiatric wards. Pleasurable infrawaves from the computer screen. Hand weapons with radiant switches. Bladder worms swimming in intestine blood. Renal capsules and tubercle lungs. Handguns with small dials. You bathe in a wide beam of sunlight. Protective screen over the biosphere. Metabolism techniques destroying thyroid health. The cold blue eyes in your DMV photo. Suicide attempt during Ibogaine treatments. You have animal intellect. You have bloodless lips. Scorched horse intestines. A close shot of your body. Your throat and tongue in a pinch. Limbs doused in mercurochrome. Swollen leaves. Exotic dancers. Chlorine undulating against humankind. You exhale talcum powder. Stealing bags of onions in the early morning. You sleep within restless oceans. Your hostile neighbors tell you they hope for social collapse, which is why they're investing in a global casino network. The US Secretary of the Treasury states there is no financial crisis. However, the economy needs a direct capital injection. An anatomical examination reveals you have skin cancer. AIDS and drug addicts in subway kiosks. You take notes from his speech. The Treasury Secretary flies out to Moscow for secret meetings. Intelligence agents ride the elevators at the Marriot Marquis. Autonomous drones pursue customers inside Prada's flagship store in SOHO. A top-level military function at the New York Public Library. In the lobby of the Plaza Hotel you hear a rude voice. Index finger releases the safety catch on the handgun. Small black eye for wearing a powder-blue pant suit. A small black box that houses a cylindrical instrument. Faint vibration from the instrument. Strong whisky held by steady hands, poured from a crystal decanter. Handgun on a wide desk. The sidewalk outside the Empire State Building. Hanging out for political assassinations. Slot machine on the back of a motor truck. Your intestinal tract filled with blood. Your intestinal waste topped with poisons. Asthma attacks abbreviated to awful cough. Pajamas worn as coveralls. False teeth inside the lining of your coat. Luxury housing inside seven-story buildings. Mammalian emotion inside the colony walls. The orb of a periscope. Needle-beam lasers fire from under the Atlantic Ocean. Smoke rises. You pour a beer into a clear, plastic cup. I swill straight Vodka from a water bottle. We sit at a table near the entrance. We share a vanilla shake. I give you a Xanax. You pass me a Klonopin. An ambulance shows up. Man stabbed in an adjacent doorway. Blood all over the sidewalk. Electronic reflex across cyborg membranes. Red eyes of a faceless evil being. Handguns. Portable lasers. Hand weapons. Low velocity tornadoes toss around dead satellites. Young woman with black hair. Impish grin under unlit candles. Automobiles beneath power lines. Sari-clad women with shoulder-length hair. Tall man meditating within a metal pyramid. President Ricky wearing a gun holster. President Ricky scowling at inter-office communications. Grey sedan cruises through thin air in nameless suburban town. President Ricky wearing a plastic poncho and linen pants. Direct light through plate glass window. Sweat stains in the hydraulic afternoon. Neck muscles of a yellowish green body. Transparent casing on carnivorous animals; their vital organs exposed. The reptilian body of fire-worshippers. Sari-clad women polishing the gun holsters of tall men. Your scowl on the inter-office communications. A grey sedan appears from thin air. You're wearing a standard poncho and linen pants. Atom bombs destroy the plate-glass window. Excessive noise. I order a drink. Another brandy. Liquor spilt on the cold linoleum. Smog over the mossy ground. The ceiling fan rotates. The exit sign with a metallic typeface. You sneeze. Hepatitis C. You enter your apartment. You spin to face me. Wrists. Elbows and guard rails. Fireworks. Oxycodone. Drug connections not subject to criticism. No more photographs in the newspapers. Bones of the dead, demarcations and formed alliances. My cleavage. Sweat stains in the hydraulic afternoon. Whole villages conduct flagellant processions of asthmatic derelicts. Your deathbed full of knives. Humans dress their computers in lovely clothes. Street hustler sleaze. Fancy prices from the coffee shop. Investigating the chest hair of your next-door neighbor. Medium close shot as the sun pours wide streaks. Slight movement as a metallic cigarette hand plunges. The housekeeper cackles. Pawned Santa Cruz skateboard deck and cigarette pack. HIV, America, drugs and pornography. Personal ads requesting liquor supplies.

Manhattan as a giant hotel room. Honeymoon suite next door to a liquor store. Huge TV and a king-size bed. An ice bucket beside the hotel door. Primary colors are the only colors on a road map. Abandoned gas stations in San Francisco. Post-humans on board the Staten Island Ferry. Cryo-patients seeking perpetual livers. I sit at the kitchen table. A compact is in my handbag. A man pounds my ass. He's deep in my asshole. He squeezes my dress off. I nod. Thick cum drizzles. You breakdown. The face of POTUS on the newsstand. Sweat pores opening inside St. Patrick's Cathedral. Space colonies being designed in the offices of the UN Secretariat Building. You enroll to study robotics at Columbia University. You purchase fabric samples in Morristown. Corpses in the roadhouse. Vengeance plans for total damnation. Hopeless agony inside an inhuman fiend. Stomach covered in cum. A large flat rock in the middle of West 54th Street. A woman's body in Rudy's Bar & Grill connected to life support equipment. A cell phone rings in empty darkness. A Ford sedan full of cash earnings stolen from Hathaway's Diner in Cincinnati, Ohio. Your celestial flesh gets midnight injections at a penthouse on Park Avenue. President Ricky on his deathbed, blanketed in knives and computers. Humans mill around him. He's dressed in lovely clothes. Street hustler making contact with secret organizations. Sleaze in the blood stream. President Ricky scrutinizing the fancy prices at coffee shop. Planets in a technological flux. Next-door neighbor parades his chest hair and garbage medallions. False reports, microfilm, personal details and glamour shots distributed in cigarette packets. The blue halo of time travelers. Lunch boxes full with lipless mouths. Magenta clouds over Manhattan. Dust swirls and spiral clouds. Your small waist. Pornographic engravings on your bathroom wall. Menstrual blood over my forehead. The private salons offering a papal kiss. Ungainly executioners staff the gaudy door of night clubs. Your fragile body-form is bedside. Physical pain and dirty floors. A scream over Columbus Circle. Hospital discloses CIA drug experiments to the New York Post. An eerie croon from mountain caves. The slim waist of hand models. The utter terror of paper dolls. Sweat as the shadow blots. Swollen carcasses in Brooklyn Hospital Centre. The vice-soaked isolation on Monticello. A hideous death and the body had black hair. You get a nightshift job and drink Chivas with spy agents. You conduct a technical analysis of the ocean's surface while I'm stuck in a cargo hold ordering hamburgers and hot dogs. Diesel fumes in the veins of a fetish model. Index fingers inside the video camera. Blunt medical instruments used as grappling spears and projectile weapons. Blowguns tied together with nylon rope. Wolf teeth glued into long-range weapons. The East River has burst its banks. Suicide of the Deputy Sherriff. The angular fragments of a read-only memory chip. The black rock formation of new cosmetics. You look at your home planet. Beasts covering the vast plains. The sexual impulse of neurotic subjects. The yellow surface of the rivers. Black hair. outside the psychiatric ward. Criminal gangs from comic books. Pleasurable infrawaves on computer screens. The fuel gauge on a dead satellite. Magenta forming within low velocity tornadoes. Your impish grin. The unlit candles of a nuclear war. Power lines purring in the night. Automobiles parked in the superdome. Brandy glasses smash on the marble tiles. You grow slimy skin, plastic scales and mossy water. You have never said a word to me. I never understand you. Rain dripping in intimate detail to the dirt floor. Police officers lean against streetlamp. You wipe your mouth with my collar. Abandoned buildings. Restaurants empty. Restaurant menus on the bathroom tiles. I wear a bad suit. I wear spectacles. Lottery tickets in a leather bag. Your shoes stop at a doormat. It is dinner time. You stare at me. Gilt chairs in dining rooms. Another sunrise. Petroleum on the beach. People pour from their homes, into the East River. Underage guy and I in the underground car park. Prisoners on Rikers suffer severe penal incarcerations, punishment. Living room. Drift-like movements. Defendant. Frozen horror. Jacket. Eyes widen. Sugar cane fields. POV from inside a coffin. Firm grip. An erection poking me in the groin. I show you my pussy. You don't please me. I wake at night. It is chilly. You try gentle persuasion on me. I'm naked in front of a stranger. You advise me to stop what I'm doing. You ask me to tell you what I see. I see nothing. Your hand disappears. I'm in the Burger King on Canal Street. I'm in my room at the Gramercy Park Hotel. I have insatiable lust for your decent appearance. You suffer with kidney and bladder disorders. Swollen joints and backache. Blanks inside the pistol. President Ricky requests his financial backer on the telepathic screen. The congregation takes place on sandy soil among red grasses. They're an uneasy mob. Beetle guards wearing hair garments. Shell-clad monsters moving with perfect precision. Strange men and unusual girls filmed indulging in backyard sex practices. Torture areas in the cavity wall. Hideous insects transforming into human beings. The natural climax of President Ricky. His penthouse floor covered in trench coats. Traffic inspectors drunk on whiskey and beer. Wine. Broadcast operator yelling through the loudspeaker systems. Antiseptics for sale at the newsstand. Advertisements for germicidal treatment. Desert sands sweep into sunken cities. Traffic accidents in the jungles. Warfare for half-dead prisoners. Nude shapes make tearless sobs. Fortress-like apartment in Washington Heights. A gas tank under the stairs. The unseen menace in a dogged drug-market. Yellow eyes, worm-eaten eyes, a mouth full of tobacco juice and toothless gums. Girl with an animal growl who works as a spotter in midtown Manhattan. The muscles of a middle-weight boxer emaciated by myasthenia gravis. Your yellow hair whipped with a silk handkerchief. Human hands in dark hallways. Your spectral fingers smeared with newspaper ink. Your body throbs with a sick feeling. At the breakfast table you detail your previous evening's warm bath. You feign emotional shock when I detail my experiences with shoe-fetishism. This is K-Mart. This is the K-Mart, Lower Manhattan on Broadway. People holed up in the Gramercy Park Hotel. I stumble around 14th Street. Close shot of your face. I'm in the lobby bar. You walk across the lobby toward the elevators. US Air Force captures alien and feeds it clear milk. You read about the stock market while wearing a baseball cap. Some company trying to turn snowballs into desert sand. Your unlit cigarette in wind. Space gamblers. Characters. VCR. Child murder. A particular book. Prostrate trees. Dead guys. Patriarchate. Quiet walls. The official masks of the secret police are left behind on the asphalt. Trains in the rail yard. Afternoon commuter service rolls out. Cars crash into taxi cabs. Taxi cabs careen into trucks. The wet dreams of serial killers. Bruises beneath your hair. Sunglasses in your coat pocket. This dignity of sex and dusk, your evil passions. Me on a patch of concrete. You behind a wrought iron fence. I feel characteristically dreadful. The sliding door to the bathroom. You previously had spent eight months in the Bedford Hills Correctional Facility. Upon your release I tormented you with an Ouija board and a hair metal dub mixtape. You proceeded to bury me in an open pit and a shovel. You wore a pentagram around your neck. I wanted to buy it off you. We disagreed about the price. Hand-drawn graffiti on your bathroom wall. It is crude. You make no apology. I don't smile. Broken windows in the lobby bar. Adrenal gland makes your whole body become weak with a decreased appetite. Paper birds upon dead bodies in dingy buildings are a contemporary burial custom. The state morgue still persists with a religious official. Stacks of stolen camera phones in my spare office. Dead flies behind the light switch panel. A certain detachment when static electricity glides upon your skin. A smooth facial mask wiped off with icy water. Denim upon clitoris. Placenta as a limp thing full of soft touching. The hotel manager talks about the old version of his testes to me. I take a deep breath as he recounts blockages inside his Epididymis. You've got sinus trouble. You give your room key to me. I head to the liquor store. I leave by the side door liquor store. Conman performs nasty tricks. All sweet talk. One hand on my balls. Government buildings in flame. People dying of starvation. I get onto the subway platform. You call me a whore. You enjoy your time in my ass. Two motorbikes leave the car park. Cum on my face. Some on my shoulders. I drain every last drop from you. Clean towels. I play it cool. You put pressure on my tits with your tongue. All dream. Vomiting again. The steel beams of the dumb world. Firemen wearing suit pants. Briefcases burning in the night snow. Dangerous instruments wheeled into the communications room. The outside walls have a wire-mesh enclosure. You inhale amyl. I purchase power tools. High class businessman getting fucked in hotel room disposes of his professional reputation. Diamond ring glints in rainy night. Chicago collapses into black mountains. Law enforcement slipping into black markets. You're surrounded with smoke, some fire simulation set off by fuse-lit grenades. Smoke and combustible materials, chemical pellets. Surface smoke. Sub-machineguns on the streets of Garden City. Fully-automatic weapons hidden in the pool halls of Huntington. Pistol ammunition for purchase in the factory outlet malls of Rockville Centre. Militant groups inhabit the manor homes of Massapequa. Automatic weapons in the Goodwill stores of Dix Hills. Contraband in the cow tunnels of the Lower West Side. 3.5 pounds of enriched uranium in a basement factory in Rochester. Templates and instruction manuals for SMGs found in a toilet cubicle at Grand Central Station. The Gramercy takes on a hot peculiar odor. A biotech conglomerate is having something called the "Pharmaceutical and Clinical Trail Awards' in the Park Room at the Gramercy. An executive wearing aviator shades has the compact smell of shit about him. Sexual instinct is now measured in blood tests and destructive gas. A mass of helicopters swarm over Manhattan. They bring torture machines that run from diesel motors. The New York Post only prints information on cyanide derivatives and the subsequent medical care if you are exposed to these derivatives. Cigarettes. Television cameras. Currency exchange. The New York Post. Extreme temperatures. I cross the East River. Buildings become wooded combs and coppices. Dreary rods of ants burrowing underground. Drag queens for every season. Long fingers in a supple mouth. An ugly gash filled with black water. An empty canoe full of metal pickets. Your shattered bones and splinters. Your titanium joints. Your cellular disturbances. Warm blood as your skirt drops. You have beautiful thighs and pallid hands. Your bare breast. You just stand there. Stirring the evening. Giant animals wander the streets. The dark evening. Hurricane winds. Motor oil on the hotel carpet. The television is on. Effective weapons held behind thick wire. Your ass wrapped in skirt-like leather. A gentle squeeze of those long fingers. A silken dress soaked in perfume. Soft flesh with black tips. On my side, curled up, with stomach cramps. Coveralls shining. Grease smeared on leg. Arms grey with dirt. Sleet rain outside. I pause. Morningside Heights. A blur of grey/orange. Woman advises me she is looking for a fight, or her husband. I buy some King Cobra malt liquor. Loose cigarettes sold for 50 cents each. I'm going to find you. The poise of your bed. A patchwork of importance. A quiet street near the Greek Quarter. My arms in the glittering air. The wind blew up Fifth Avenue. The next morning I slept late. NYC full of big trees, rather pale-looking. Overcoat shining with oil. Your tattooed arms grey with dirt. A blur of aged and orange muck. Wallpaper covers the walls. The sensual heaviness of a smooth cranium. The telephone psychic tells me she has measles, little spotty pus things on her skin. We fuck in a public park that's down a small side street. A butcher knife leaning against war trophies. Crates of pepper spray and metal batons hidden in the deepest part of the Okefenokee. You design a safety mechanism for homemade pipe bombs. Steel slivers in the flesh of your palm. Smokeless powder on your tongue. Yellow teeth caused by excessive liquor. Loaded gun discovered in the ballpark. Shrunken heads uncovered in Manchuria. Loaded gun pointed at the magazine photographer. Strange girls in the theatre foyer. Press agents conducting radio interviews. Fan magazines full of celebrity pictures. You're a lifelong bachelor. Loaded gun in your slender palm. Fingers bent backwards. Desert sands of Arizona. Cactus over the flat landscape. Elderly man with neat curves. Matchhead shavings that cause nausea. Nerve gases provide temporary disorientation. Poison gas pumped into the Applebee's in White Plains.

Bare breasts, panting against your skin. You stand there. Stirring the evening. Giant animals wander the streets. The dark evening. Hurricane winds. Engines up on cinder blocks. Motor oil on the hotel carpet. Television on. Plastic outdoor furniture in the kitchen. Sun-warped. Cracking. Peeling. You're not seeking any publicity. Tequila inserted into apple pie. Common talk in a prison scene. Your bloodshot eyes and a dirty neck on a park bench. In a soggy basement beneath a Superdome you heard sacred music. The cash register works for advertisements. Desert sand on your bare leg. Dirty hands around a gas lamp. Murder scenes inside private prisons. An idea to put an above-ground railway through Koreatown. My thought repeats. A scramble of bodies across the bar at the King Cole, St Regis Hotel. Toxic urine splashed against the urinal. Cab drivers in the taxi rank on 96th Street. A wardrobe of women's clothes. Custom's regulations published in the New York Post. Existence alternating as alien. I can't work anymore. Footsore. Hungry. Thirsty. I shake my head. A hair lock on flesh sliced from leg bone. Outdoor chairs stolen during home burglary. Murder committed as a non-political crime. In your top drawer is a small capsule of poison. Clay sequestered in secret rooms. Your soft smile in a moonlit field. A deep dark shadow as sweat forms a sheen. Shock treatment destroys your new brain capacity. Intelligent citizens morph into dysfunctional leaders. Radar screens set up in storm drains. Sewerage full of gutter shit. Refugee compounds as endless makeshift cities. Sex changes on Wall Street. Ice box full of Chivas. Dishwasher gloves draped on radio speakers. Luncheon service dishing up cobwebs and artificial grass. You rack up cocaine lines. Ear canals burning in post-midnight reverie. Late 1980s Christianity warning against contracting herpes. Game show contestants featured in news reports. Studio lights affecting television crews. Buddhists admit to being religious beings. Tweed coats. Television audiences dressed in animal skins. Tobacco smoke classified as a viral disease. Fly screen windows damaged during prison riot. Capitalist bosses grinding on the nightclub floor. The Togo Government props up its economy with bootleg sales of Armagnac. A golden sun above glaciers. Dark forests on the Himalayas. Andes full of ice field ranges. Unbreathable air discloses whimsical dialogue. Efficient patterns engraved upon impressive terrain. The Chief Zoologist fucks the Radiation Specialist. Time Machines for sale on West 45th Street. The Vietnam War fought between Russia and Korea. Free brochure advertising glamour photography. Radiator pumps imported from Mexico. Exotic girls with blood red hands. A civil war in Mali. An economic depression in Sierra Leone. Atoms and molecules form the ionosphere breaking apart over Midtown. I watch pie charts in a PowerPoint presentation. Sample products of perfume on my skin. Human blood on the pillows strewn. Robot in a metal shell. Tiny wires in a giant mechanism. Ember fire on a lit river caused by small incendiary bombs. Your measureless boredom. Sadness envelopes as you watch the corpses wailing. The electrical impulses of a giant moth. Your desire to undress in Tompkins Square Park. The death rattle of a hypodermic needle. Cargo boats on the Hudson. Your thinning hair caused by valve leaks. Your bare hands on a demolition bomb. The trademark torture of the dead. Blood trickles in the snow. Nude bodies in the bathhouse. Earthquakes from pre-historic times shipped inside dumpsters via Atlantic City. The onset of a world war due to a cold war between the Eritrea and Ethiopia. Killer is now the temperament of humankind. Tweed-clad Cosmonauts shipped in crates to NASA c/o the Lyndon B. Johnson Space Center in Houston, Texas. Alaska is now the only country in the Northern Hemisphere. Staten Island is now a VIP area for a wide array of rare women. Exotic smells from the Bronx are investigated by the NYPD. Billy clubs smash out the lights of Broadway. GIFs with the images of bloodied jungle floors. Blowgun darts dipped in potent neurotoxins. Woman accuses NYPD of gross negligence. Cab driver disseminating soviet propaganda. Corruption causes medical experiments to go wrong. Medical personnel perform head shavings on patients. The dehumanization of persons, the technological implications. Assassination devices for sale on Canal Street. Handgrips and tobacco pipes. Official checkpoints full of paramilitary weapons. Trench knives and brass knuckles. Bayonets and sawed-off shotguns. Metal tubes filled with pocket clips. Teargas cartridges among radio antennas. Crude mechanisms with coil springs and elastic bands. Pistol grips. Metal tubes and pipe fittings. Automatic pistols with violent recoil. Your trigger finger. People holed up in the Gramercy Park Hotel. I stumble around 14th Street. CLOSE SHOT OF MY FACE.

I'm in the lobby bar. You walk across the lobby toward the elevators. I don't smile. Broken windows in the lobby bar. Potential bottlenecks on the Lower Manhattan Expressway. You're in a dark suit, standing by the window, the door closes. The sunlight outside blinds pollution. You're in a pornography booth. A bitter aftertaste in your throat. Confidential papers in a manila folder. Acid daylight dissolves before tomorrow. The marvelous intellect of the Commissary Manager at the Rikers Island Correctional Facility. Cops with lung problems. The chief financial officer for a real estate company in Manhattan has been arrested for exposing his penis in a public lavatory. You're interested in the incalculable harm his life has become. Hell as dark blue rain. Radiated engineers asleep in roadside hotels. The correct information on your death certificate. Trench coat twists in wind. Deep sigh in the background. Someone listens to Stryper. Cigarette smoke, my throat feels rotten. Electric motors manufactured in South Carolina. Caskets assembled in secret shipyards. You're at the loading dock. You deal in body parts and ESP. I look at the decaying bedsheets. Your slight insanity. Your cloth nightgown. Your bedsheets. MED. CLOSE SHOT – your face, it's light and dry. A car door slams, camera in my hand. A midtown hotel refuses me entry. A musty-smelling hallway. I breathe in. I have a psychic condition. Tiny bedroom. Black depths. Box cutter. The hyper-realized sense of tangled highways. The Seville Motel in North Bergen is a lump of masochism, physical restraints and self-inflicted wounds. A tight spiral of steady whirlwinds. Elected officials in rattan suits.

Bonfires in the twilight air. Snapping warmth. Flames burn Grand Street. Grease in intestines. Gray and orange muck floods Wilmington Avenue, then continues for a twenty-block radius. Every subway train and gas station is closed. Every convenience store window is damaged. You hid cigarette boxes in your soft black hat. The streets are littered with milk cartons and candy wrappers. You sit and watch it on playback screens. You hooked up with a local kid who had a hash pipe. He worked for Amtrak, but would constantly call in sick. You were bored. You threw a party and that night we all kneeled around the makeshift altar. I disconnect the saline bag. I look at the IV lines. I look at my cigarette. You feed me food after you were released from the Bedford Hills Correctional Facility. You get a job running weed all over Manhattan. A phone screen inside a large hall with an impressive stair way. You jot down descriptions of male genitalia. Helicopters over Morningside Heights. Wooden crosspieces on the outer walls of sex shops. Dance floors installed in all toilet stalls. I ingest your perfume vapor. There is complete silence. The dull repetition of human figures. The internal mechanisms of the laboratory working overhead. Air currents clockwise spiral. Peculiar clouds seep into the control panel. Chemical affinities scar your long fingers. Neat moustache hides your sour personality. Sea levels and nose bleeds. All average citizens garnished with oxygen masks. You wear triangulation glasses. A yellow dot on space charts. You enter the bedroom with an exquisite feeling that ends in languor, convulsive spasms and fungal ingestions. Air hangar doors close. A wood cabin with a warm bed. A tape measure in a paper bag. Polyester drapes in a hotel room. A metal bucket beneath your bed. Effective selling of acid in Washington Square Park. Dry limbs on hairy chests. Prosthetic eyeballs and latex fingertip attachments. Pewter castings and flesh-blinding powders. Caustic substances that cause permanent blindness. On my side, curled up with stomach cramps. Coveralls shining. Grease smeared on leg. Arms grey with dirt. Sleet rain outside. I pause. Morningside Heights. A blur of grey/orange. Hollow tubes and open pouches. Hollow tubes and aerosol canisters. Non-toxic substances mixed with sulfuric acid. Plutonium dust amongst anthrax spores. My thought repeats. A scramble of bodies across the bar at the King Cole, St Regis Hotel. Toxic urine splashes against the urinal. Cab drivers in the taxi rank on 96th Street. A dark age of short dialogue. Septic abortions in the guest bedroom. Comatose patients administered on the night shift. Bartender stares. Tarot cards putrefying beneath the exit ramp. Pick-up truck in the rear-view mirror. Skin inserted into a cremulator. Automobile and wooden boxes behind stone wall. Your hand slips from my thigh. You're watching airline flights from the cocktail lounge. Shortwave radio broadcasts over car radio speakers. The unhealthy oil of corpses. Sarcastic smiles in the bedroom. Beer smell permeates the carrion stench. Nine minutes from the end of summer. Plastic bag full with unclean teeth. Your body in hot summers. No money exchange at La Guardia. Air-conditioned sleep. The high temperatures. You stroll across the tarmac. I show your boarding pass to the steward. Her face is disjointed. The steward gives me a free washcloth. Solitary confinement. In the Manhattan twilight I stroll. Suicidal symptoms. R&B on the car radio. Your cold right hand in a tropical climate. A brandy and dry with a rub of dirt in it. Wooden mallet against window pain. Chemical nucleotides removed from the bodies of dead soldiers. Meat delivered to the penthouse. Growths on the soil. Creatures in towers. Animals across the skyline. Wine served in plastic cup. Fingers found on the desert sand. Cigarettes on asphalt. Your ligaments and toenails. Your sideburns and palms. I sit here quietly, thinking of nothing in particular, women's clothes. Stick figures eating hot dogs. You place the handgun in the drawer. A traffic intersection. The light remains red. Nothing is relevant to the picture I see. You shake your head. I have a prescription for Seroquel. We collect the production stills and various PSI data. I get hit square in the face. You attempt to sell me an insurance policy. Everyone in the taxicab beside us has their heads bowed, their hands clasped. I look at a street sweeper from various angles. The oversized wheels. You and I are flesh-to-flesh, eye-to-eye. We should've rented a car instead. Underage boys procured for secret police. A coastline of condoms, rats and ultrasound assaults. You cum, clean and change clothes. Another person plants their cock inside me. Two frantic homeless men fuck and choke me. It's your problem now. You expect your clients to be strange men. I think you're a kind man. I disrobe in front of you. It's your time to swallow it. A wardrobe of women's clothes. Custom's regulations published in the New York Post. Existence alternating as alien. I can't work anymore. Footsore. Hungry. Thirsty. I shake my head. Lap dance for executive staff at the Pitt Consol Chemical Company. Commuter's cutting across the Calvary Cemetery. Drinking Brandy in a taxicab as we cross Kosciuszko Bridge into Queens. Commuter's faces. The bricks, cement and wood of Greenpoint. Rodent-like forms and insect creatures. Primitive worlds with superior races. Alien minds with upper-level evolutionary sequences. Blunt fingers on your right hand. Sea levels and open mouths. Cold nerves inside time travel. Red curls over shoulders. Green eyes analyzed by language enthusiasts. Intricate equipment engenders field reports. Transparent bubbles full of pale parasites. Clouds over the driveways of Maspeth. The propionate unity of your body, a particular shape underneath a fake fur coat, the real distinction of alabaster, your hazel eyes. Your fake fur coat stinks. Fur tufts in a gravel road. You collect $3.50 an hour. A gift shop inside your right ventricle. Airplanes descending upon LaGuardia Airport. You head straight from your Comfort Inn to the train station. Space capsules landing on Europe. The vatic significance of cocaine. That classless essence of suicidal depression and shame. You uncover the beautiful cabalistic truth from the secret police, the US intelligence community and ordinary assassins. Toxic substances and miniature knives. You have multiple punctures on your forearms caused by thumb daggers. Handguns left on hard surfaces. Children's novelty items sold by black market dealers. Long baton made from an aluminum rod. Your metal knuckles around my neck, strangling me. Foul-smelling skeletons prized about with kitchen shears. Aquatic lizards below clay fields. Moisture in the soil. My boyfriend with a flat voice. Coin slots to gain access to city toilets. An old man kills his young assistant. Your mediumship tapers as you place fabric samples on my forehead. Vicious dogs on the Great Lawn, their nerve endings and mucous, their frayed membranes. Your helpless date smokes tobacco from a Belomorkana cigarette through a water pipe. The geologic porosities of Pepsi-Cola. President Ricky on your laptop screen. Body bag over the shower door. Brush fire on the windy shore. The forensic expert with broad shoulders. New gadgets for the city jail. The retina hollowness of the cyborgs. Celebrity images and glamour shots as a GIF. Upstairs you ask me questions as the scorched-out city teems with snakes. President Ricky finds himself in a savage place. The soft drink dispenser now distributes the silicone required for fake breasts. A wet skirt covering your right nipple. A male with many tongues in his mouth; his main tongue resembles a slimy growth. No more intelligent life, no more intelligent beings. The vast expanses of colonisable outer space. Opportunities for local girls in Vinegar Hills to make offal. You get rid of your extra skin. I check out surgeries online for you. Medical practitioners asleep in their waiting room, asleep under the coffee tables. You cry blood onto a comfortable pillowcase. The procedure is expensive. We discuss working the system. How do we game a body-contouring practice? Close-up of your sharp nose. Black forms fondle galactic microforms. Mountain range in the rearview mirror. Alien air minus gravity. Earth oxygen encrusts smooth-worn boulders. Strange clouds seen through your field glasses. Wide panoramas of featureless cylinders. Air currents and thermal chimneys. Strange invasion of telescopic eyes. You are not a welfare recipient. We purchase a scalpel. I enjoy being the center of attention. You put your cock tight inside me. You look at me embarrassed. You're usually meaner. You rip out my blonde hair. I'm too weak to fight. The synthetic appearance of the elevator button. The mild thrills offered by a dark-haired dominatrix. Cigarettes and gender roles. Cigarettes and wind over the milky asphalt of Ninth Avenue. The official masks of the secret police. Trains in the Fresh Pond Junction. Afternoon commuter service cancelled. Cars, taxicabs and trucks clogging the Gowanus Expressway. Drug use in the mental wards of the Mount Sinai Hospital. A sadomasochistic affair in the hotel room next to mine. Growls of vanilla sex. Emotional support in a hospital hallway. Restroom sinks in an emergency room. Jehovah Witnesses dousing their brain cells with massive doses of smart drugs. Shivers and moans. You ejaculate twice. My breasts. I mention that you would be fun to go shopping with. I lay on the mattress after you fuck me. You tell me I have put weight on. My arms are scabrous. You ask me to massage your legs. You don't give a shit about anything besides my asshole. You survey the lunch menu. I sit down and wipe my lips. A napkin. You pull me between your legs. Two people dressed in random-looking, cardboard cut-outs of themselves. Semen like melting lard. Information processing during safe sex, cheap thrills or other contaminated sensory inputs. The intimate snugness of your figure in a Balenciaga Bandeau Bodysuit. Post-humans on the Staten Island ferry. Television screen in the carpark. Urine on the bathroom tiles. Blood beneath Williamsburg Bridge. Phantom vessel in the East River. You polish your stainless-steel appliances. Off-duty army people working in factories. Cigarette stains from the river streams outside. A man stabbed eight times. I saw it. Left when the police arrived. They arrested the killer a few weeks back. Cryo-patients with haptic perception. The elevator arrives. Attorney pulls out a tube of Acnomel Adult Acne Medication. Attorney rifles through your suit jacket. Coffee cup and a pregnancy test. Attorney grabs a block of cedar wood. U.S. drone strike campaign against Afghanistan, Kandahar, Dubai, Mogadishu and Somalia. Your attorney smells like American cheese sticks and perfume bottles. A police officer slaps me across my face. Hollywood celebrities in Norway. Cigarettes in the computer library. Intelligent life inside a cloud mass. Red dots on a long slope. Sensitive mortals with abrupt impatience. Loose sleeves on your old sweater. This hot planet with its acid tongue. Your pale eyes looking over tundra of small rodents. The greenish iridescence of your huge eyes. Your brain records reconnaissance methods and the wire enclosures of NYC. You throw my body on top of the table. You slap me again. You swallow me. You smile. You're on the TV. You pin your lips to mine. I walk three blocks to the mall. You top off my ass. You feed me snacks. I sweat something fierce. Nipples all over my body. You pound my ass again. I can't walk. Torn blouse. You step back. You rub my groin. Red raw. You push me through the doorway. You masturbate. Scientists with lean features, brawny mouths. You fill out several questionnaires about the state of your finances for an interior design firm. A destructive childhood spent in SOHO, New York. The eye-catching ways of a gangling fellow collapsing on Roosevelt Island Tramway. You stub your big toe in the foyer of the Walgreens on West 4th Street. You conduct stem-cell clinical trials while wearing the silver high-heels usually favored by eccentric tycoons. The medical reporter notes that for professional reasons she categorizes homeless people into either Earth-type or Alien-type planets. The rain is cancelled. You sit back on your heels. Slowly erecting are my nipples. My weeping groin. I am topless. You force your cock inside me. Sweltering nudes on the sofa devouring ass. You work inside my ass. Tight-fitting. Green mucus. Blood. Cum. Eventually the pain breaks me. Alone on the bathroom tiles. We snicker. Urine in tumbler glasses. I am angry. I smash stuff against the walls. I kick holes in the wardrobe doors. I want to chop off my hand. Cut out my heart. Pizzas with triple toppings. The lips of your future lover. Secret experiments behind massive doors. Police uniforms for sale in the retail shop of the Mercedes-Benz Superdome. A smoldering fire put out by inpatients at the New York Methodist Hospital. Your body behind a shower door. On the passenger deck floating into New York Harbor. The cacophony of year zero. A stable job even though your life has been spent drunk. The formal qualifications and intellectual mutations that make up your past atrocities. The environmental damage caused during your future atrocities has been given a dangerous rating by the USEPA. Agricultural menace. A packet of sugar on the dresser. You hunch over, snatch my backpack and run. A middle-aged woman looks at me. She ices her voice. I look at her. She's up. Running. Peeling off into tide. Into her room. The woman looks old. Metallic typefaces on subway entrances. Outlandish motion. Fidgeting. Twitching. Get me out of here. Florida destroys all its fireproof buildings. Silicone materials are replaced with champagne. Puerto Rico is relocated to the Pacific Ocean. The murderous work of the napalm nations. Fragmentation bombs destroying frozen jaws. The military objectives of the human conscience. You piss in the winter dirt. Drunken girls make dark jokes. Ancient buildings under brighter streetlights. Attractive limbs smothered in Irish Whiskey. The soft rush of your tight pants. Pubic hair on an Indian rug. White mice underneath a glass tabletop. A coke spoon in your pocket. A photocopy of your criminal record in your briefcase. Your long legs over mountainous terrain. Great insanities in the jailhouse. Prosthetic tongues created by batch spawn. Electricity cut to the Old Quarter. Toothpaste on your white shirt. Coat hanger on the bathroom tiles. Heavy luggage on a bathroom scale. Laundry starch like light sandpaper. Your car furnished and expenses paid. Face surgery after accident investigation. Naked CEO fucks senior citizen. Earthquake in the Gobi Desert. Plus-sized package with correct postage. Cartoons with Infographics. Standardized exams for sexual research. Death medicine for monthly repayments. Junk food for Africa. A bread roll spinning on the hotel stairs.

Drawstrings undone on my pajamas. You pick my pajamas up off the floor. A man pounds my ass. I trim my pubic hair with a cigarette lighter. You're up in my asshole. You roll off me. I nod. Thick cum drizzling from your cock. You breakdown. POTUS on the newsstand. You talk enthusiastically about shampoo and conditioner, about giving me a scalp massage. Underage guy listening to Paula Abdul's greatest hits. My skin started to peel off, most of the muscles fell onto the attached floor, looking like a water cardboard pancake. Great cities of South America. My eyelids shut. I stand up. You grab a fry pan. There is yelling. Shouting. Shrieks. It's feverish. Your life put together. A jigsaw. All shucking and bargaining. Scabs on your forehead. Weed smoked in a Chick-fil-A carpark. Parasitic shudders as you exhale. All rituals are observed. We're in the underground carpark at Willoughby Square. I show you my nipples. The TV screen. An erection poking inside me. I've never killed anyone before. Your apartment is packed with too much furniture. Stacks of sewer pipes and dollars. I sit. On the TV an anchorwoman is narrating a wildlife documentary. She shuffles some important papers. She places them in a floor safe. Food and animals and the obliteration of the world outside. I think I might want to purchase a fast-food franchise. You're in an empty space with your right hand. The camera follows you in a gesture of utter contempt. I read about certain mathematical tests of randomness. I then read about a homicide investigation in New Jersey. Darkness knocks me to the ground. I show you my pussy. Your expert hands. Your mouth. My groin. You refuse to please me. Ambulance crashes on Whitestone Expressway. Soft warmth. Silent gasp. You retrace my steps, limping among the wounded, dreaming while daring, torching the quiet places. You pull a knife on me every two hours. I look into your eyes, your face turned out. Your cheeks indifferent. The cab door opens, You step out, your expression is tin-tacks and glue, maudlin. Blonde hair. Toilet paper. Money. Oral stimulation. Pussy. Mind reader. Small containers. Cum. Body limp. Hard flat stomach. Favorite pussy wrapped in surgical gear. A young man wears a green coat. Your tiny cock is a pitiful excuse. Photocopied advertisements on an electricity pole detail cosmetic procedures to assist in male enhancements. Washboard hands make you a pleasure giver. You're naked in front of a stranger. The stranger states they have a kinky side. I'm hungry. I go downstairs and get a burger and large fries. Charcoaled dogs on the sidewalk. Lunch on the subway platform. The stranger calls me a whore. I told him he couldn't choose time inside my ass. He leaves on a motorbike. Torn t-shirt inside a carpark. Cum on my face. I drain every last drop from your cock. Clean towels. Your tongue in numerous bowels. Feet that look like liver. Hair in your mouth. Your middle finger at the camera. Muscle in your knees strained. Shop girls making appointments with stupid boys. In California desert, you meet your close friends in marble halls inside an industrial park. A vague idea of my arms locking together. A painful recollection regarding the dried bicep of my left arm. Polaroid sunglasses and secondhand watches. Jeweler and radios in your water closet. Stereo sets and cookware in your wardrobe. Silverware and hunting equipment under your bed. Glassware and linens in a suitcase. Drapery and fabrics on the furniture. Toys and fur stoles in the laundry. Hosiery and assorted clothing in the shower stall. Shoes in their shoe boxes. You fuck in the empty countryside. The CEO of a major oil company constructs steel-like muscles. He craves lifeguard shoulders and athletic legs. Office workers on 32nd Street drink synthetic beer. Dollar bills in plastic containers. Airplane trips over the Atlantic. Homeless students in Portugal. Young men wearing patent leather boots engaging in mutual masturbation in the dry docks on Port Jersey. An imitation rubber penis wrapped in red silk. Your phone number written on the wall in public toilets. I purchase black leather boots from discount department stores. I play it cool. We're on the escalator at the Best Buy on Lexington Avenue and East 86th Street. Pressure on my breasts from your tongue. All dream. Vomit. The alcoholism of the underage guy. Our weekly arrangement. Two frantic homeless men fuck you. They choke me. I disrobe in front of them. Discreet staff in the private change rooms. A bottle of special moisturizer. You take time to swallow me. You massage a little moisturizer into me. Scratches on my thighs. Hips and stomach. Your round hand. You kiss me. Future generations of peasantry. A narrow skull full of blue fluid, intricate cylinders and platinum sockets. The national press prints editorials written by young anarchists and power freaks pushing a skinhead opinion. Voluntary censorship in Abyssinia and Italy. White fibers on a hairy body. Throat that swallows your dark eyes. Long fingers around ugly tower blocks. Dismal streets covered in reddish dirt. Buildings made from brilliant stone. Light flashes through the Lower West Side. The derelict ships of modern society. Slight smiles on faces. The engines purr. Body armor in the hyper-tunnel. Weird things on life support. Styrofoam cups full of animal sperm. Dire warnings on LCD screens beside the FDR Drive off-ramp. Thermometric bomb broken to pieces. You cum before me. You bring the body. You're too lazy to get up and clean me off. I have no energy to resist your temptation. I'm in the toilet cubicle next to yours. Bottle caps snapping loose onto the tiles. Lubricant. Deodorant up my nostrils. Lingerie in the wastepaper basket. New people with new feelings. Effigies as apparitions. A blue hairdryer placed upon personal papers behind a glass partition. Porn movies screening in your stairwell. You get solitary confinement for consecutive life terms. Cum in your saliva. Condoms and green mucus on the sidewalk of West 124th Street. Greasy glassware manufactured in Rwanda and Haiti. Practical lessons and specific models derived from economic disasters. The pendulum between a non-sustainable course and the cautious optimism of a new romance. The miniature sensors inside your time machine. Small blood vessels smoked in carbon dioxide. Your esophagus filled with stomach acid. Bikini briefs beneath your nylon jacket. Your sequin breast. Gasoline savings in the latest Chrysler. Laboratory tests for shampoo hair. Soppy lather on your toothbrush. Skin disease and heartburn. Adhesive tape on your hypodermic injections. Press releases for illegal sound. Major oil companies with seasonal layoffs. Accident investigation with no gimmicks no charges immediate delivery. Easy monthly payments and wholesale discount prices. Electronic equipment for cancer treatments shipped to England. The plastic electrodes of the stimuli machines. The headaches and mathematical instructions of a bad trip. Gunmen shot in Pakistan. A U.N.-backed polio vaccination drive in Karachi. International aid work focuses on the major food shortage and refugee crisis. Modern pirates need expert advice on how to conduct a civil war. Machine guns and car traffic. One of your more laidback interrogations. Examinations interrupted by lines of cocaine. Scar tissue over your ribcage. You eat a French steak. Laboratory with dishes of biologic mutations. Lightning outside your apartment now. Windy streets. Vertebral fractures of the outside world. Scrapbooks of coding. News clippings in your wardrobe. You pull the deadbolt up and open the apartment door. A brown-haired man enters. He places a hundred dollar note into my palm. He has large breasts. He's more interested in my ass. He pinches my ass apart. Africa as a difficult video game. The dust, steel bodies and scraping glass of modern warfare. Apartment blocks with apartment doors. Cab drivers escort police officers across town. Manure smells on the Gowanus Expressway. Manure smells in Manhattan Valley. Car keys left behind in NYC phone booths. Giant spaceships ascend from modern worlds. Sizable islands sinking into vast oceans. The aromatic pain and beautiful warmth of seawater.

Your busy fingers over my body. The lascivious abandon and sensitive organs of young men. Fingers on the remote controls. You assign me a submissive role. Coarse massage oil on your hands. The center of Manhattan. Mid-morning. A young woman bedding a teenage boy. Tiny microprocessors conducting illegal imprisonment for perpetrators of DDoS attacks. Persistent rumors regarding the supposed homosexuality of the POTUS. Phantom vessel in the East River. Radio plays R&B while I polish my stainless-steel appliances. Manikins in pencil skirts. Off-duty army people working in factories. Visual aids and miniature travel packages to Argentina. Brutal ideas. Serial killers in your wet dreams. Chemists working in warehouse. Rental properties south of Harlem. Bruises under my hair. Electrical energy sourced from Brazil, Bolivia, Chile, Paraguay and Uruguay. There are no lone shooters – only MK-ULTRA. Cigarette stains from the river streams outside. Large breasts all booze-lined. Your pussy as a lame gift. You tear at my blouse. Buttons on the linoleum. A new load into my ass. Underage guy covers his head in sackcloth. I pour Visine into my Mountain Dew. Rectal bleeding in the shower stall. Nausea attacks. A teen party for freaks with malignant diseases. Pizza delivery cancelled throughout Manhattan. Death certificates issued automatically. NYC as post-industrial war-zone. Psychotic children with deep anxiety. Gas station robberies and movie theatres with a violent language. America in slow motion. Your minimum wage job. McDonalds throughout Mexico. Tent cities in a recession economy. Financial blowout causes extreme blood pressure. Resistant bacteria in your Gucci loafers. Parasites in your cigarettes. A heavy smoker with sunburn. Extracts from citrus trees causing defective skin pigmentation. Tooth decay as a birthmark. Expensive gambling in Israel. I'm sound asleep. Inside the Edison Hotel. Guts and hips. I have caught some rare disease. Let the game unfold. You scream. My jaw pinning my tongue against your skin. Your asshole stretching too fast. You make me cum. A man stabbed eight times. You saw it. You left when the police arrived. They arrested the killer a few weeks back. You exit your own body. A stranger as an insurgent leader. Forensic expert purchases your body behind a shower door. Windy shore attacks by a brush fire. File cabinet in the main office. Mutual consent to kiss our broad shoulders. Tattooing needles inside the Lincoln Correctional Facility. I'm in the main office waiting for the late arrivals. Hot plate on cornea. Wire in the iris. Aluminum foil pierces the ciliary lens. You head to your hotel room. You remove your coat and put on a hanger. You toss yourself onto the bathroom tiles. GOP leaders at Dorrian's Red Hand. Hollowness inside my retina. Side effects of medication. You fuck my ass. Myriad TV screens with advertisements featuring soda and low-calorie snacks. Ice-covered facial expressions on game shows. I need a haircut. Hard cock inside me. Cock enters me. Condoms in my coat pocket. A packet of Telecine. Laser beams over rooftops. You wish to slow dance then saddle me up. You fuck, then finish me off. I reach for your vagina. You clutch it. Scratches on your torso. Subway stations. Your legs twisted painfully.

My body. A new plan in my brain. You insert your hands into my ribcage. You tell me what to do. It involves my ass. Commuters tarnished in unhealthy oil leaking from Bayway Refinery. Cyborgs patched together with discarded pieces of plastic. Contaminated water in the New Croton Aqueduct. Thousands of dollars in plastic shopping bags. Clinical studies on children to determine appropriate dosing. A yearlong war. Breath tests. Empty sequences. War mercenaries. Your cingulated cortex. A crowd of three hundred. B&W photographs in your fireplace burning. A terrible riot inside Times Square. Blackjacks cracking over heads. Incurable psychosis. Crude stimulus of alcohol. Skateboarders dodging slug pellets. Retina hollowness. Commuters, Unhealthy oil. Cyborgs. Corpses. My juices. You rub cum between your fingers. Underage guy puts antifreeze in my brandy. The shower stall. You smoke weed. We walk to West 124th Street. Your breasts in cum. I force your body off me. IBM super-computer in your basement. Gene therapy with your mistress. Physical acts in unsafe structures. You're a full-blown masochist. S/M in the piss-smeared nights. Recreational therapy with stimulating images. Letters to the editor. In the Gramercy Park Hotel, you watch television. You're everything like it is now. Calm. Useful. NYPD looking at us. My throat. The change room door. A janitor wipes the window. Cigarette smoke. Silence. A woman comes to change the linen and towels. She has hives. You're driving our new hire car. You take the corners funny. The world doesn't look any different. Your tone is that of a prosecutor. You make fingers movements in a gentle circular motion. Spotlight inside your bedroom. A cherished memory permits you to smile. Nothing. A great explosion. You walk toward me. I can smell the aftershave. Your stubble. You're wearing a tie pin. You check my name. No San Francisco appointments penned in. No slots on the computer screen. You tape a knife to my hand. You extend your hand. You give me a bath towel. Nothing else. My stomach filled with alcohol. Animals whipped with four-inch leather straps. I open a tobacco box with bruised thumbs. No one has slept. A surgeon at the NYU School of Medicine skols aperitifs. A plane ascends of the skyline. Students run from the school. Photos on an adult online magazine. President Ricky with a perpetual diseased liver. Sweat pores in Astoria. New dimensions to the apocalypse. Silver coins in exchange for superfoods. Stock prices collapse. Babysitter kills toddler. Your vagina is all dark and unshaven. My waist. Saliva on your face. Palpitations. Gut pain. Dry mouth. Testicles in front of stranger man. His face rough. His hairy crotch. His sarcastic smile. Old brown hair. His legs straighter than mine. His thick cock. Bicep on his left arm. My breasts sweaty. Your long black hair. His right hand. My inspection of his body. His dirty hands. My whole hand into his wide lips. His amazing pussy. Beer on the card table. You read every medical journal that mentions implants. You take tomato juice to your plastic surgeon. He talks about the atom bomb and smiles. Electrical impulses stored in the kitchen drawer. Fingers over hot bodies. The head doctor smears cream onto an old man. The old man is bent over a long narrow table. His raw pussy. Large-b/

small-c cup breasts. I give you a blow job. I am thirsty. Sweating. Vomiting. Diarrhea. Underage guy on a grappling surface. Hard bodies. My tits get crushed by a local boy's cock. Cold air bruises my behind. Double attack on my anus. You drag a fingernail over my hole. Zeroing in on my rectum. We cum together. Wet appetite returning. You massage me for fifteen minutes. Outer ear. Earlobe. Eardrum. Enzymes. Male cousins. Sarcastic smile. Bedroom. Laboratory. Titanium joint. Tubing. Replacements. Sterile pigs. Cocks. Burn pathology. Hospitals constructed from wood. Light bulbs. Great steam. Field conditions. Beauty salon. Unspoken caress. Anger. Bathroom tiles. NY harbor. I spin around. Basic plan to clean out the brothels of NYC. Cell phones and bootleg cologne bought on Canal Street. Your face purified from plant sources. Your indifference to medicines prescribed for you. Tufts of smoke present in subway entrances. Tarpaulins over statues of war heroes. Throbbing. Burning. Steamed mirrors. Radioactivity. Animal and insect experiments. Heaps smoking. You cum all over me. Half-aroused. Invisible puppet strings. Your fingernails in my mouth. Campfires. Coyotes. Human bones. Teeth. A bottle in my anus. You embrace me. Pinched nipples. Underage guy lifts my skirt from behind. Condoms burns in dusk. Puffs of steam. Unpleasant in our street. Small toe. Right foot. Sex acts. Salmonella poisoning. Seroquel. Bromine over my eyelashes. Photographs of your stark flesh. Shrapnel dissolving in your skin. Ordinances. More empty sequences. You smoke tobacco beside a wire fence. Gossip columnists trailing your social exchanges.

The creviced tones from your mouth. Blood plasmas. Blood pigments. Respiratory enzymes. Blow-dryers in the latrines. You play cards during the bomb scare. Graphic sexual activity within suburban house. A large river of hot ash. Water bottles smuggle teeth, blood and cool drugs. You cover yourself in deep mud during the nuclear testing. The telepathic thoughts of gunshots. Satanic sessions commence in the late afternoon sun. Non-smokers purchase condoms and alcohol with dirty money. Your broken finger holds the automatic weapon. The cigarette smoke from an off-duty attorney. Cellular disturbances. Brown skin. Superb creature. Masterful husband. Warm blood. Skirt drops. UFOs now classified as 'religious weapons'. You sleep wrapped in influential newspapers. Weekend parties with packages of LSD. Shoe leather in your mouth. Asleep in the Gramercy Park Hotel. Asteroid belts and complex organisms. Medical researchers whose blood drizzles. Slaves with shrewd eyes. Deer-like creatures in the shadows. Unwary beasts in protective suits. Beautiful thighs. White hands. Funeral. Oppression. Exhaustion. Water. Park Avenue. America. Midnight injections. Celestial flesh. Central nervous system. Washington Bridge. A lean black man wearing a Soviet Army officer's cap. California has a peaceable nature. You need to fix past mistakes. A snowbound car with crystalline feathers in the trunk. Imprisonment in part-time different jobs. The shower curtain in your fingers. You've spent multiple lifetimes in your complete image. You wear black stockings. Nail polish spilt on your lace brassiere. You spend the summer months residing in official agencies that offer twenty-four-hour emergency services. Jungle floor. Pepsi-Cola. Laptop screen. Glamour shots. Cigarette packets. Investigation committee. Personal details. False report. Microfilm. Applicant reports immense unidentified visuals over Morningside Heights. A summer afternoon. You pull out. Your half-aroused cock sprays over the bedsheets. The hotel holds large rats. Blow dryers belt out heat. Card games in the lobby. Insatiable stations of HIV. Bodies stormed by tortuous corpses. Bones all grey and gold. East River Park. Streetlight. First Avenue subway stop. Reading the New York Post. Outbreak of contagion in NYC. Hula dancer tattooed while on probation. Your neck contains tiny metal filings. Jackboots upon air bubbles. The vulgar nebulas of NYC nightlife. Alcoholic drinks while listening to radio transmissions. A male juvenile attempting to light a wet cigarette. Perfect husbands. Subnormal intelligence. Possible progeny. Abnormal circumstances. Potter's Field. Various stinks. Café. Electricity pole. Nakedness. Libidinous feelings. Psychic focus. Paris. New shoes. Morbid reluctance. Cut-off gloves. Fingers stroking. Windscreen. Car stereo. Rolled-up sleeping bag. Paper cup. Police force. Dark blue suit. Severity of faces. Fifty alkaloids stolen from Walgreens. Youth serving as soldiers. Bayonets flashing in the land around Dead Horse Bay. Blood on my stockings. Water-filled lungs. Echoes. You're face down on your stomach. Motionless. Steam pipes on the brick wall. You scrape about on top of me. I arrive at the office and laugh. You have brought a shotgun along. You place it on the bonnet of the car. You order pints of Brandy. My thigh is bruised. You put your gloves inside your coat. You fall from your chair. Sunrise. Fresh air. I look pale this morning. Porn magazines in picture frames. Ashtrays are cluttered. You have never said a word to me. You drop to the dirt floor. You ask me to stop what I'm doing and tell you what I see. I see nothing. Your hand disappears. You retrace your steps. You pull a knife on me every two hours. I look into your eyes, your face turned inside out. Your cheeks uncaring. The cab door opens. You step out, your expression is tin tacks and glue. Maudlin situation. You head to your apartment. You remove your coat and place it on a coat hanger. You toss yourself onto the bathroom tiles. Black oil on the frosting snow bed. Your forefinger and thumb turning amongst mould. You chain smoke Bridgeport cigarettes. The surface of the East River, cum-soaked and brain-dead. Your liposuction performed on car seat. Police chief on public radio station. Flat tire on automobile. A fierce fire through NYC. A plastic cup from the Vatican. FBI members taken hostage in Lear jet. Skiwear shop in subtropical regions. Purse snatcher drinks alcohol. Blood congealing in the bathtub. Foam and cotton towels. A skeleton of bones, yellow spots on your skin. Water against the embankment. Tall crests. Robust undertow. Health department rejecting discourse and intellectual atmosphere. University President experiences light-headedness. Anthropologist with a restless mind drinking a bitter espresso. The steady flow of sugar upon the riverbed. Empty chairs at the adjacent table. A vacant seat at the student hangout. Politicians on surveillance video. Seroquel on a summer afternoon. Evil smile on subway train. Large brains transported in bedsheets. Blood on the side of a lifeboat. Hurricane winds lifting from the street. Dark reveries. Musical notes. Oven door. All-American World War. Dark stare. Comfortable perch. Window bay. Tragic event. Sonorous tones. Flat voice. Amazing theory. Reportorial. Killers. Journalistic standout. Left hand. Coat lapel. Murder case. Voiceover. Police methods. Hotel room. Moisture. You walk into the living room. You pick up a magazine from the coffee table. You browse through it. It's a medical journal. The American Journal of Transplantation. Surgeon pitted against surgeon. You pick your favourite implants. Barbed wire from the kitchen drawer. An electrical impulse runs through your hand. You demand pain. Molecular studies. Girl. NASA. Porosity. Sciences. Secret police. Killer. Russian invasion. Repulsive voice. You snicker. You quickly retrace your steps, limping into the lobby alone. You wear a t-shirt. Your car comes to pick me up. This is the second times in a few hours. Neurologists and pharmacists conspire to place you in The Tombs. Your face all turned out. Your cheeks full of yellow piss. A cab door opens. You stroll along Orchard Beach. You sniff shoe adhesive. You pat out your lit cigarette. I am in the hotel lobby waiting. I glance sidelong at a shot of Brandy. Abstraction of the wounded dreaming. Brick wall. Boyfriend. Flat voice. You fall on the bed. You kick the nightstand away. Shoe leather fills your nostrils. The concierge gives me a blank cassette. We're eating hamburgers outside the telephone box. The inner earth has a new sun.

Every species stampedes. Your tears descend. Your lungs expel the dust. Sunshine against my wet ribs. Your footsteps descend. My eye implodes. The clapping sun sweeps across the city. Veins burst out of the river creatures. You eat a chicken nugget. We enter a second-hand-clothes store. I rub my ears with my new coat. Sweat stains. My thin body tightens. Toy soldiers for sale at the gas station. Back at the motel. Your bare buttocks and full lips in the big shower. You were someone's husband once. Blood drizzles from a wound. Flashback. Evil genius. Fire. Seminal weakness. Starvation. Religious reference. Sunglasses. Graffiti. Hand-drawn. Crude. Abhorrent. Apologies. Swine. Rattan suits. Infantile. Mistakes. Iran. India. Russian heartland. Dreadful divinity. Garbage. Eyes. NYC. Laboratory specimens. Jehovah. Kitchen area. Acid. Bass line. Hot summers. Physical sense. You pull a knife on me every couple of hours. My toothbrush in your bathroom. The tears of your eyes. My tubby neck. Men pierced with tin-tacks float in the Hudson River. Foul-breeding snakes hatching in the Arthur Kill. I am shoeless. You extend your arm and guide me to sit. Homemade universes. The sand dunes on Fire Island. A woman squats over the pavement. A hurt woman with sore breasts. Long black hair in sharp photographic images. Unforgettable moments from these distant years. You take long absences to delve into deep thoughts. New machines on the Trans-Manhattan Expressway. Homosexual boys fuck the cruel bridegroom. You like mischievous laughter. You undress out of a black dinner dress. I wear your high heels. Light through the ventilating shaft. Scalpels into the skin. Destruction of the body with every body blow. Robots run for political office. Professional men tear down their immoral past. The possibility of fire hazards. An embankment of stones, almost a levee, holding back the seawater. I need to substantiate that the handgun is still in the drawer. A uniformed cop on the doorstep. You burst out of the door, running clumsily. I'm nuts for you. We stare at each other. Your wrists and your ankles. Participants to the computer program. You gently kiss me. You tell me about your financial problems. Deceptions that you believe. I believe you. The computer operator inputs comments. A black flat-brimmed hat. I'm out on the staircase. I'm listening to the city. I look at my ticket number. Bedrooms and living rooms of NYC. Weed smoke among the rooftops. A Mercedes in the airport garage. You twist your hair curls. Your body from my tongue. You restrain me on the floor. Sweat forms on my skin. I catch a glimpse of life and passion, a forever condition, they then administer brain implants. The alcohol was delivered before. I take a sip. Knives in the penthouse at night. Homosexual publications. B&W sketches on a KFC placemat. Skin blackened from drug addiction. Headaches. I'm in the corner, standing alone. You're exhausted with excitement. I walk toward you. I draw the handgun. Shoot a bullet into the drain, into the center of some embers. The steward puts a hand towel over my nose and mouth. Hand towel is soaked in Vodka. On my knees. Flesh ripped off. Consumption of blood inside a steel chamber beneath Fulton Street. Muscles under x-ray. Excruciating traffic in Manhattan. Scrub bush as overgrowth.

Woodlands in the Lower East Side and then Financial District. Sunken streets outside supermarkets. Rusty water in CVS pharmacies. Moonbeams on a dark evening. The psychotic symptoms of traffic cops. You put your face on. The NYC dawn is analgesics. Electrical states inside your head. Rail tickets printed with ink. Time. Snails. Bus stop. Smoking. Right hand. Cool climate. Anti-pollution. Killer. Long life. Human ideas. Hard power. Hong Kong. Deep ultraviolet rays. You get me back to the hotel. White shirt tight against your chest. I'm burnt up. You open your mouth. Moss and plaque and dry toothpaste. "Make sure you clean them in the morning," I tell her. Turkish men. Long lifetime. Vantage point. Useless genius. Ex-psychic. Naval aid. Asteroids. Meal token. NYC. Complex organisms. Blood drizzles. Captive slaves. Shrewd profile review. Kitchen help. Servant eyes. Coffee table. Double bed. GIF. Wax effigy. Requests. Scum. Fresh victim. Coffee table. Medical journal. Poisons beneath your skin. You wiggle your behind. Hurricane winds hit Manhattan. You sob in the pale dawn. Backseat of my car filled with soggy boxes of anesthetic. Bony disorder in a shirt sleeve. Deliria. Substance abuse. Alloy pushed into circle shapes. Medical charts held under spotlight. You push yourself against me. Her face in my pressed shirt. I make it to the taxi, tight traffic. I don't want to meet anyone. Open sun sitting in grease. People fumbling with street rubbish. You talk in patronizing statements about dirty concepts. Your words are unique, yet difficult to determine. Aberrations. The hurricane winds. Implants. Plastic surgeon. Plastic surgery. Kitchen drawer. Electrical impulse. Decrepit merchandise. Emotions. Unsafe. Large balloon. Tire smoke. Hydrocarbons. Intelligence training. Empty sequences. Secret police. Short walk. Specific doom. Solar system. Galaxy. Earth. Time travel. Nose crinkles. Deep breath. Woman. Listless. Hand. Uruguay. Time travel. Time travelers. Blue halo. Cigar smoke. Men without external sex organs. A sliced penis and scrotum in a coffee cup full of endocrine. Southern mansions repurposed into abortion clinics. Old photography stock. The swamp. Idle machines. Amoeboid bodies penetrate various large cities. Warm flesh throughout humid NYC. Air patrols and the National Guard. Spider creatures squash the Pentagon. Hot pistols of reddish dust. The quiet air of radio communication. The white walls of the lavatory. Skeleton foot in the slippery washbasin. You leap from the high window. The sick cold air. The sparse hairs of tree limb. Conventional sex positions during measles. Dense cartilage floating within ocean currents. Your saliva is bone-dry. Cheerless disease on the airport tarmac. CIA staff with hypoxemia. You put your face on. Woman outside sobbing in the dawn. Bath soap smells like tree sap. Burnt hair clogs the sewers of New Orleans. Electrical storms. Asian boys. The open sun of New Orleans. Hurricane debris. Paramedics seek psychic help while emergencies revolve around them. I feel ill. Bone materials. Wounded people. Beer and tracksuit pants. Signs. Skull housing. You ignore me. Withdrawals. Traditional symptoms. Your skewed eyes of slumber. Transparent messages. Your dampened glare. Dosages. Looking through the drawers for cigarettes dipped in PCP. On the roadside a dead body. Shreds of epidermis. A scar around your eye socket. You go on blind dates. Wind, soot-like, full of rain. You believe your body will become dirty. Caterpillars and rodents in the subway station at Lexington Ave/53rd Street. Vast stretches of escalators. Commuters transferring. Expression. Question. Atmosphere. Scenes may induce psychotic symptoms. Boxes of anesthetics, analgesics, anticholinergics. You book two airline tickets to Donitz, London. Me in disorder, coughing up chunks of wet bread. Ink on my shirtsleeve. A man in a suit giving out tiny pamphlets. The sound of your voice is unique and difficult to determine. Killer. Musical works. Ghetto. Sudden jets. Musicians. Gene expression. Time-tract theory. Important points. Historic decision. Time travelers. Rimy smirk. Black guys. Odorous tirade. Eyewash. Nervous system. Riot. Andrew Dice Clay. False molten center. Elemental residue. GIF. Peyote buttons. Cheeseburger. Hologram. Twilight. Hospital. Doctor. Out-of-date Coca-Cola. Heavy tobacco. Different meanings. Feeble lips. $300 in my pocket. Fortnight-old fried chicken. Light bulbs flaming. You're out-of-breath. Steam in the subway. A limited range of feelings. You're on my body in this horrible afternoon. A common afternoon. An electric cord full of oil and cigarettes. Stupid dreams from the morgue keeper. Special investigators with their high-octane corpuscles and black eyes. You draw a deep breath inside the subway. A 300 pound monster is up for execution. A flashlight beam on shoe leather. Upon the pavement a shrill whistle. The rough tug of a t-shirt from your shoulders. Children on the basketball court. We're here to book the Honeymoon Ballroom. The car in the scrap yard is on fire. I lean over and kiss you. You graze your elbow on the tiles. You light a cigarette. Exposed blade bone and bloody tampon. Beauty salon near West 207th Street. Your tongue on the envelope. Bonfire in the 191st Street subway station. A police officer assisting you into your bed. A temporary trash dump, bathrooms towels rubber-stamped with your initials. Rubbish cooking inside garbage bags. War-like acts. A boy. Songs. My belly bulging in animal fat. Plastic bag caught on barbed wire. The uneven rhythm of your high heels in the empty corridor. The disinterested voice of the elevator man. Your large brown eyes in the small mirror. Common slogans rolled out for a new social drug. Passport stamps required for space navigation. The decipherable faculty of the human ear. Light aircraft carries prosthetic skulls and genitals. Blood of your kidney and shin. Microscopic films detail the future civilizations of interplanetary space. Rail yards built in Morningside Heights. You roll up your sleeves. You've done these scars yourself. Sunburnt troops storm into New Orleans. Lacerations and drunkenness, absurd news updates on the radio. Fairy floss burning in turpentine. You open the door to the Ballroom. I recommend you go see a health professional. Banknotes billow in the parking lot. I enter the parking lot. I recoil violently. You grab my arm, sweat spurting from your face. "Have you heard these descriptions of me?" The photograph of my body is a disappointing mistake. Photographs. Photographer. Service contract. Suburban home. Police fire. Atomic bombs.

Rubbery leaf. Frantic warnings. Concave surface. Giant stems. Shrill whine. Graceful antennae. Tight girl. Right nipple. Common tube. Large breasts. Wet skirt. Right nipple. Main tongue. Cold air. Biker guys. TV personality. Strange man. Money. Medical researcher Directions to a big island. Galactic trade agent. Bizarre experiment. Colonies. Zen experience. Wall Street. New race. Replacement hips. Tobacco. Cocaine again in the bathroom. Cubicle closed by shower door. Soap in the shape of jewels. Soap taste inside mouth. Dogs patting sex dolls. Hair locks. Fresh eggs in the bee hive. In the next five years, our bodies will fall apart so much that we'll be able to bring every grey morning inside us. Hand sweat on rock walls. You're asleep in small boats. From your back muscles, sweat pours. Machine-like precision to destroy you. Magazine publishers talking to television stations. Cadillacs, Chevrolets and Chryslers appear from murky blackness. Spiral staircases all throughout Chicago. A morgue team collecting cell organisms. Electronic diathermy in a large town's orphanage. An insane gleam to your eyes. Bodies shudder with showed intentions. I resort to thoughtless action. Asleep. Faces inches from the way the dying bird struggles. Wings clipped. President Ricky walks into the living room. She picks a book up from the coffee table, she browses through it, it's a medical journal. Plastic surgeon pitted against plastic surgeon. She picks her favourite implants. Barbed wire from the kitchen drawer. Eyes so gentle. Your ears and ass are lost. I examine your pelvic muscles. Rope around your ankles. Your eyelids are translucent. Testicle sweat in your hand. You're all raw-boned, sharp-cornered and skinny. Paranoia. My uneaten sandwich. Bottles of water. I've been keeping secrets in my head, all of them, intended warnings, excitements of escaping, a living tide around me. It's not until eleven years later that I think about being homeless again. Fires on the outskirts of NYC now. Electrodes connected to unexplored planets. The new version of NYC is to be supplanted into South-East Asia. Eyebrows torn from your face. Plagues pour from distant boroughs, foreign lands. The urinals smells like perfume, vomit and shit. Decomposed hot dog buns. Water snakes covered in sand dunes. Snow falls on a bus stop. An electrical impulse runs through her hand, demanding pain. I hike up the hill. Sailors annoying me with deck chairs. Index fingers snapped in two. Parody of real self. Gentle vitamins in sewerage system. Glass windows shriek and carve brightest statues. The paint colour is ridiculous. Convenience store at night. Suction cups on male nipple. Soap dish in shower stalls. Chest hair over medallion. Telepathic screens. Deep breath. Incredible orgasm. Key ingredients. Women's washroom. Stomach muscles. Body shook. Sweat patches. Pleasure. Long nasty. Woman's voice. Enhancement breakthroughs. You sit at the serving table. A general food cart swerves, it tips over. Ashes of wood, plutonium rods in the refrigerator. The light of the kerosene lamp. Flesh underneath the railway overpass. New technology. Warm cum. Surgical capabilities. Bony fish remains. I pick you up from your hotel room. You strip down to nothing. You tell me you're not going to hurt me. You offer me something to eat. A voice through a loudspeaker. Sodden snow-driven ground. A nightmare world of endless new condo apartments. The quiet disaster, considerable fun playing in the nuclear reactor. Polar icecaps melt, solar radiation, the clay walls of Queens. The moon base holds space animals. Staten Island is reduced to amoebas and fat bellies. Condensation on my lips. You work in a huge office inside the New York Times Building. I wear a miniskirt and leather jacket. You're in disciplinary mode. The t-shirt slogans of egotistical children. We look at rental properties. You have a sloppy tongue. Bruises where the blood stops. I need a hospital. A busy street. I'm in a $119.00 dinner jacket. Semen stuck to my jaws. Spaceships ascend. My abdomen covered in haversack. Plasma leakage from arteries. Cardiovascular collapse. Semen over your pajamas. You tell me that I'm rather nice to you. A pick-up order of Chinese takeout. I've just awoken. I pull lace garments from my body. Starvation. I want to head overseas. Anywhere. Peace found on ocean sleep. Hands in a sweating pit. The present imagery is inspected. A new amount of soreness inside my head. A portion of your tears, a piece of salty mulch. You're in the shit. Your drunkenness. Your hair tresses. I yell. Total stasis memory as I sit on your water sofa. The cushions ripple. Valves. $59 for a new bottle of perfume. Brain technicians ebb out onto the street. You're average height. You work at a hardware store. You have fine features and tiny breasts. You're in my underwear. Alluvial deposits at the Sims Municipal Recycling Facility in Brooklyn. The Atlantic Ocean accommodates your narrow body. Turning pages of The New York Post. You pour yourself a glass of beer. The sky stoops in a darker blue. A peculiar complexion on your face. Rattan suits all careworn. I wait for you in the hotel lobby. A boat out in the harbor. The harbor water is transformed into unmarked and sensuous materials. Your lips in a full-length mirror. Indifferent to everything. A doormat. Loading docks. Light in the dumb TV show. The stock markets without cocaine. A wide array of call girls. You were found unconscious in a field at sundown. Parking lots. Sewer ditches. Drowsiness creeps over Manhattan. The youth are greased for sex.

Shane Jesse Christmass is the author of the novels *Belfie Hell* (Inside the Castle, 2018), *Yeezus In Furs* (Dostoyevsky Wannabe, 2018), *Napalm Recipe: Volume One* (Dostoyevsky Wannabe, 2017), *Police Force As A Corrupt Breeze* (Dostoyevsky Wannabe, 2016), and *Acid Shottas* (The Ledatape Organisation, 2014). He was a member of the band Mattress Grave, and is currently a member in Snake Milker.

Made in United States
North Haven, CT
26 November 2022

27222399R00064